100 Bug Doodles

by

BeastFlaps

BugDoodles.com

for my son

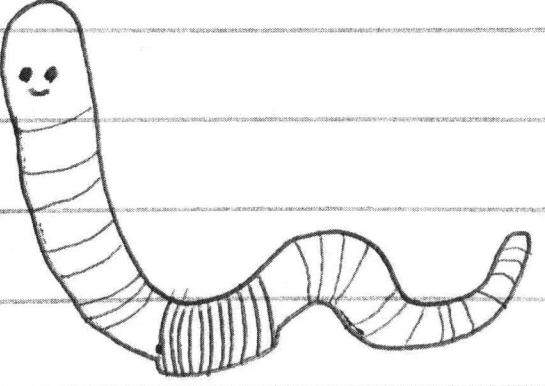

IF YOU COULD BE ANY SUPERHERO WHICH WOULD YOU BE?
DUDE, YOU'RE LITERALLY SPIDERMAN.
@Beastflaps

MOM I HAD A BAD DREAM! CAN YOU CHECK THERE ARE NO PEOPLE UNDER MY BED?
@Beastflaps

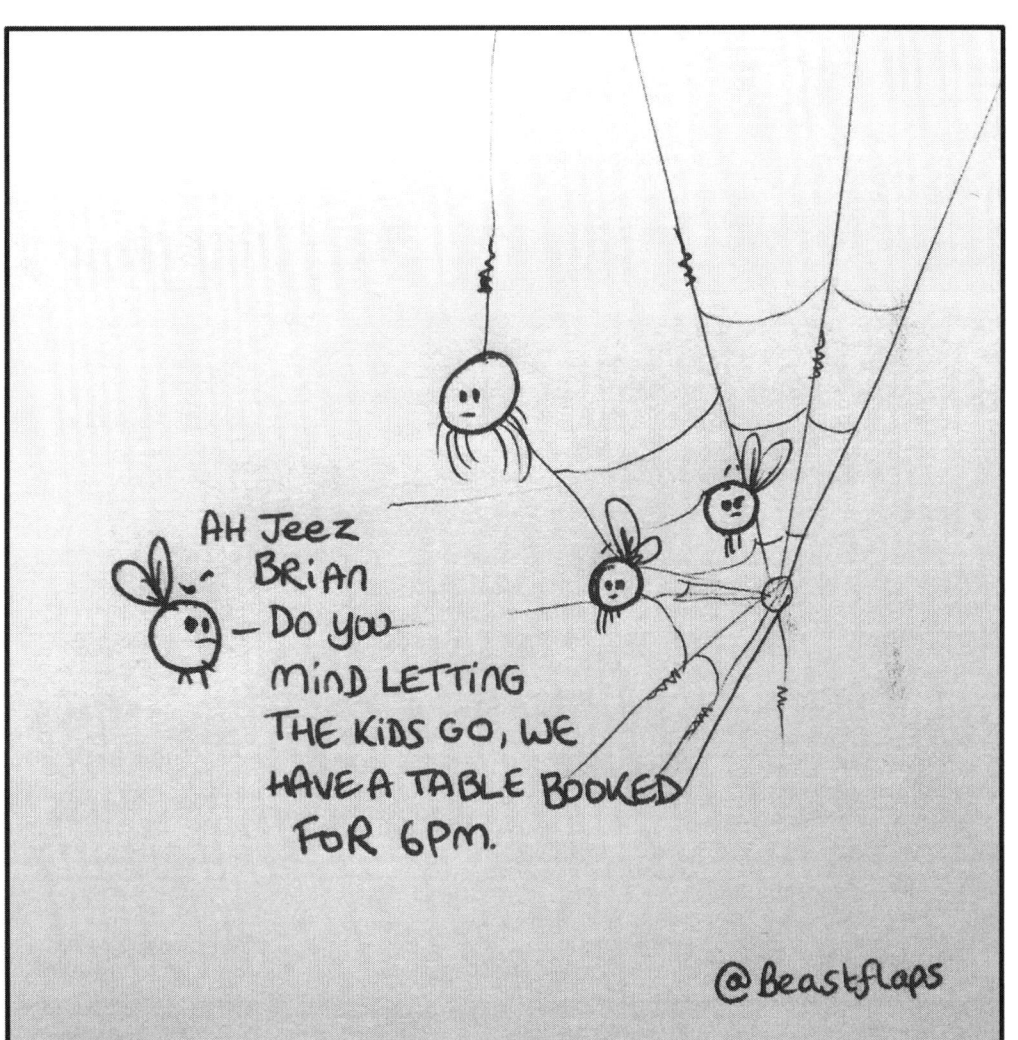

WHY IS EVERYONE SCARED OF US ANYWAY?
IT'S BECAUSE THEY IMAGINE MY HAIRY LEGS CREEPING UP THEIR NOSTRIL AS THEY SLEEP AND DANCING IN THEIR SKULL.
YOU'RE NOT RIGHT IN THE HEAD DAVE.
@Beastflaps

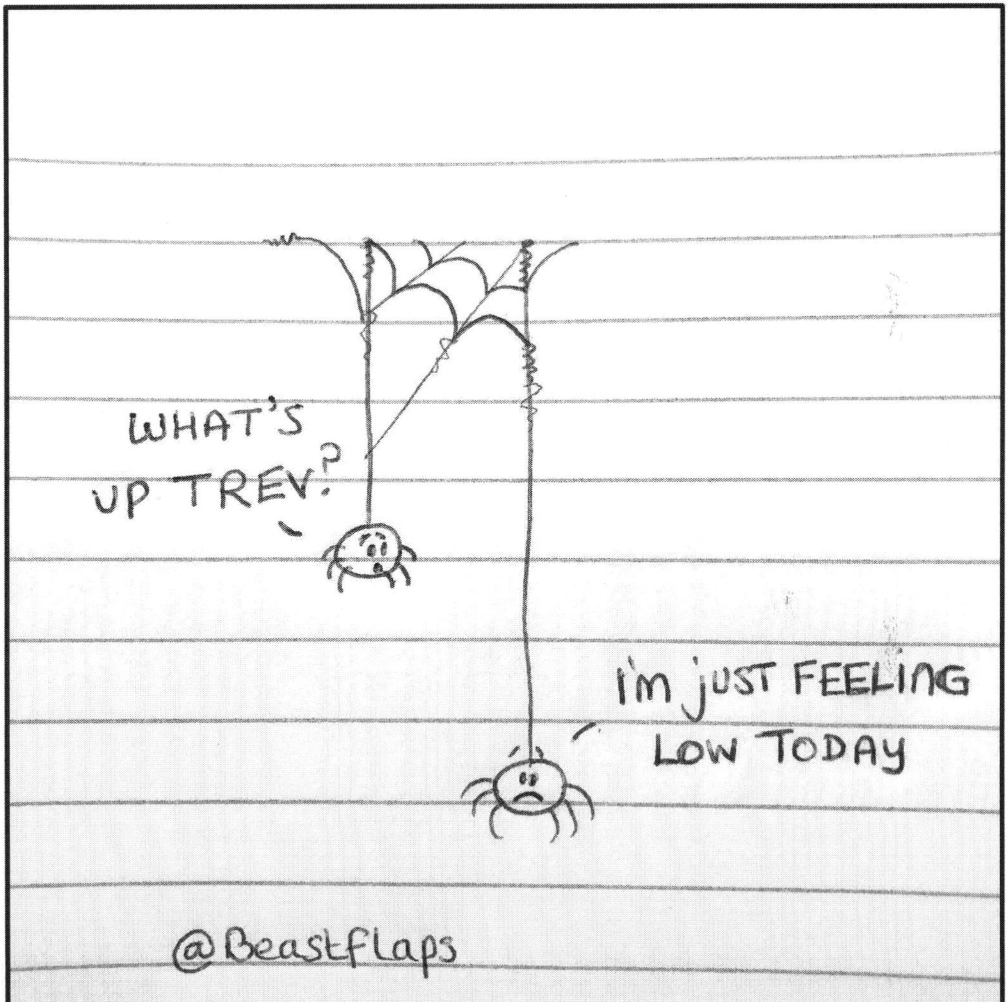
WHAT'S UP TREV?
I'M JUST FEELING LOW TODAY
@Beastflaps

"WHAT THE FUCK TERRY, YOU CAN'T JUST COME HOME WITH BLOOD ALL OVER YOU AND NOT EXPECT QUESTIONS."

@Beastflaps.

DON'T YOU SOMETIMES WISH WE COULD JUST TAKE A NICE RELAXING WALK?
I HAVE NO IDEA WHAT YOU'RE TALKING ABOUT
@Beastflaps

LIKE MY GRAMPS USED TO SAY:
"IF AT FIRST YOU DON'T SUCCEED NOBODY GIVES A FUCK, YOU'RE JUST A FLY."

@Beastflaps

WANNA START KEEPING FIT?
MARY, WE LIVE FOR LIKE 28 DAYS
@Beastflaps

@Beastflaps

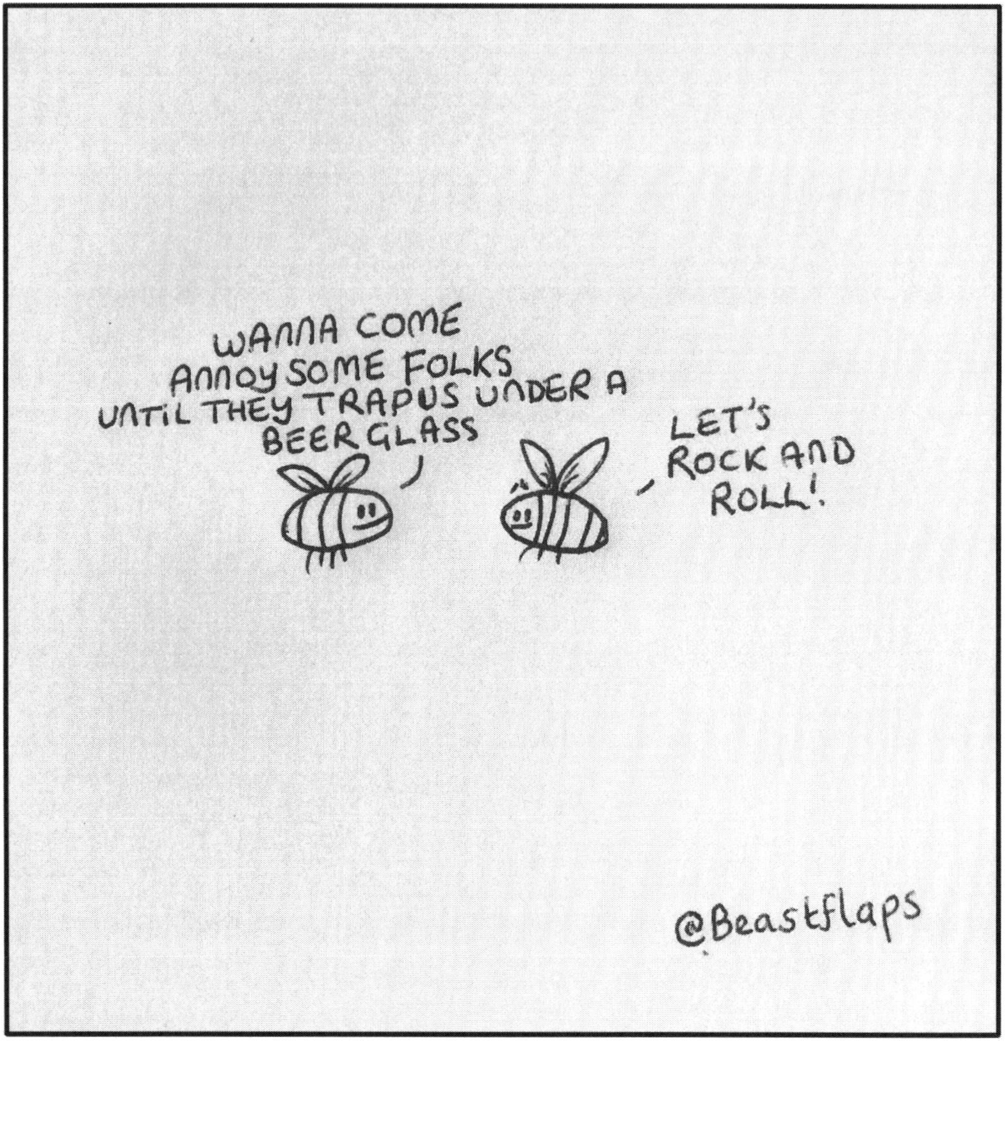
WANNA COME ANNOY SOME FOLKS UNTIL THEY TRAP US UNDER A BEER GLASS
LET'S ROCK AND ROLL!
@Beastflaps

TERRY, WHAT THE HELL ARE YOU WEARING?
YOU SAID WE NEEDED TO BE MORE CURRANT
@Beastflaps

MY INSIDES JUST BECAME OUTSIDES. IS THAT A GOOD THING?
@Beastflaps.

...!
READY! COME FIND MEEE!
OH MY. I WONDER WHERE HE COULD POSSIBLY BE.
@Beastflaps

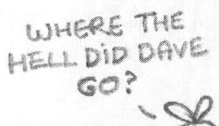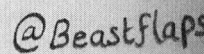

Now vomit it BACK up
SO THE HUMANS CAN EAT IT.

@Beastflaps

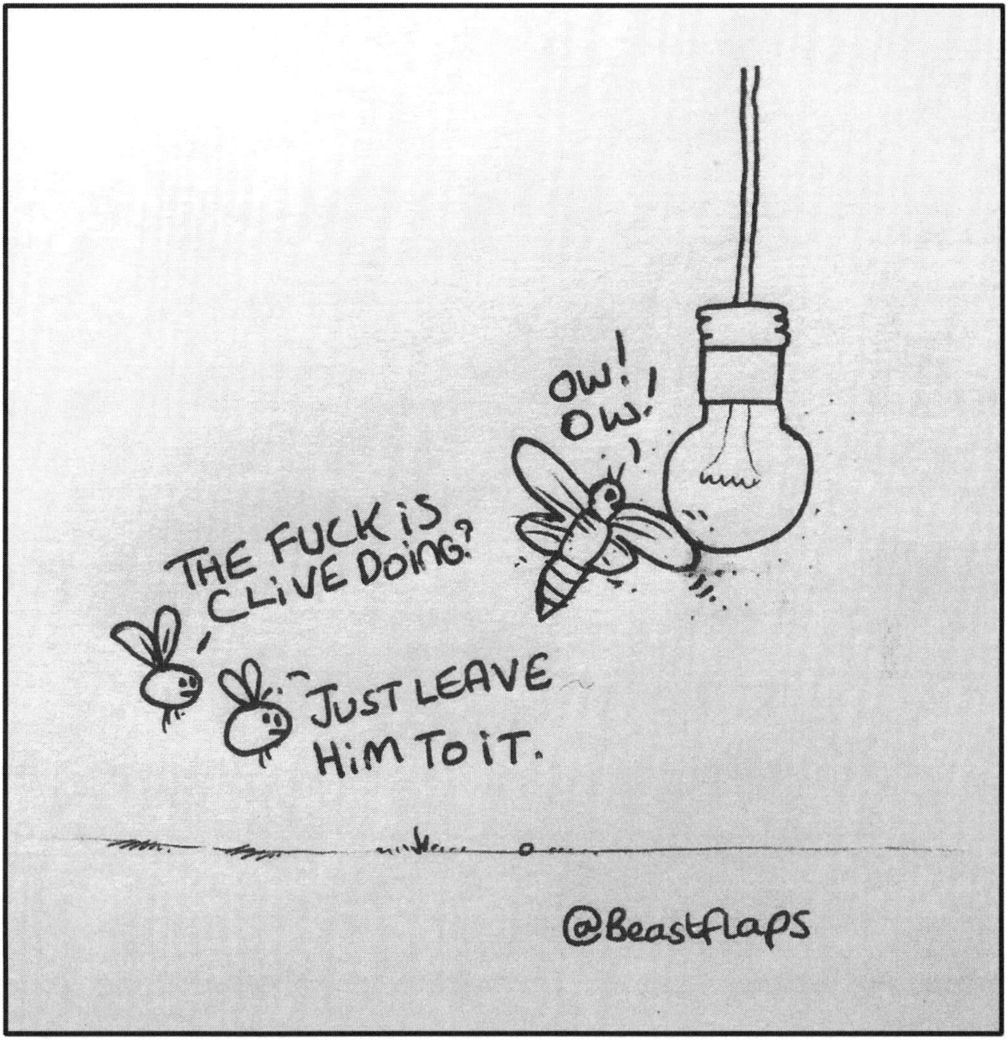
OW! OW!
THE FUCK IS CLIVE DOING?
JUST LEAVE HIM TO IT.
@Beastflaps

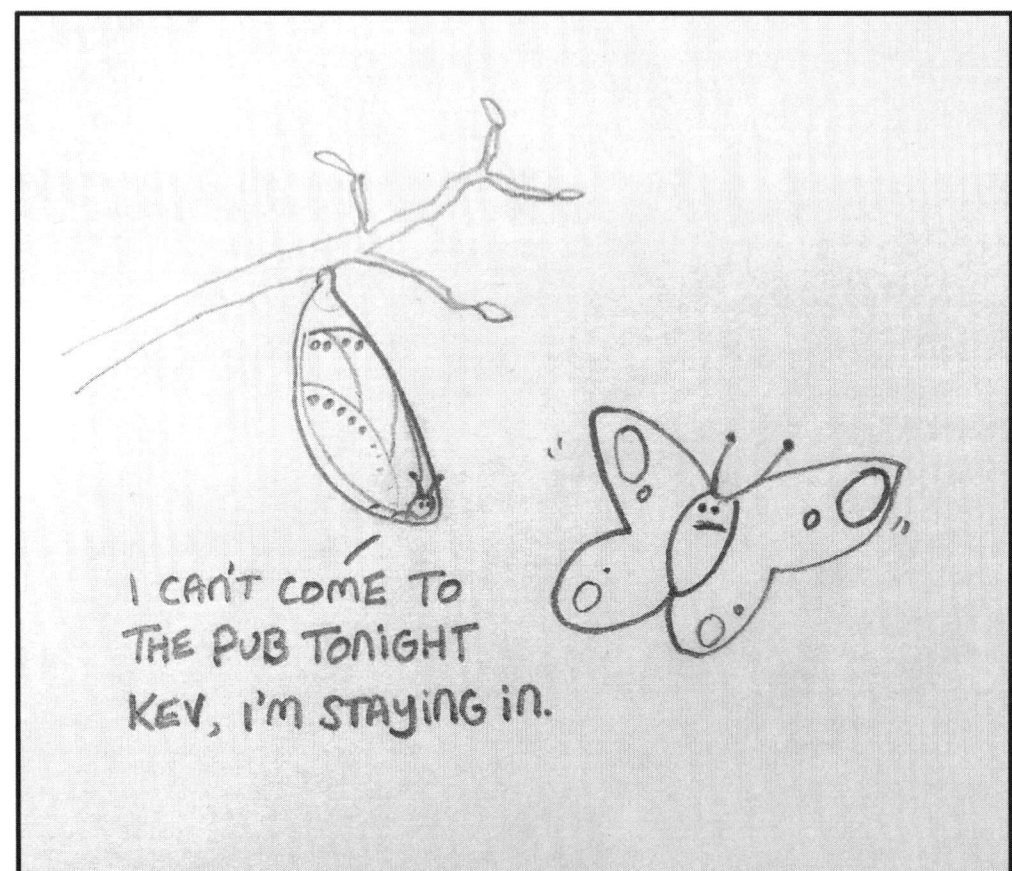

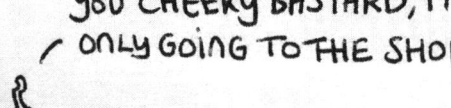

THE EARTH IS FLAT, I'M TELLING YOU
KEITH YOU'VE LITERALLY NEVER LEFT THIS BATHROOM
@beastflaps

THE SICK FUCKS TOOK HIS WINGS! THEY TOOK HIS LEGS!
THAT'S A RAISIN DAVE.
@Beastflaps

DON'T MAKE ME GO BACK in THERE, IT'S FULL OF CREEPY COBWEBS
Yeah, i'm PRETTY SURE THAT'S ALL YOU STEVE
@BeastFlaps

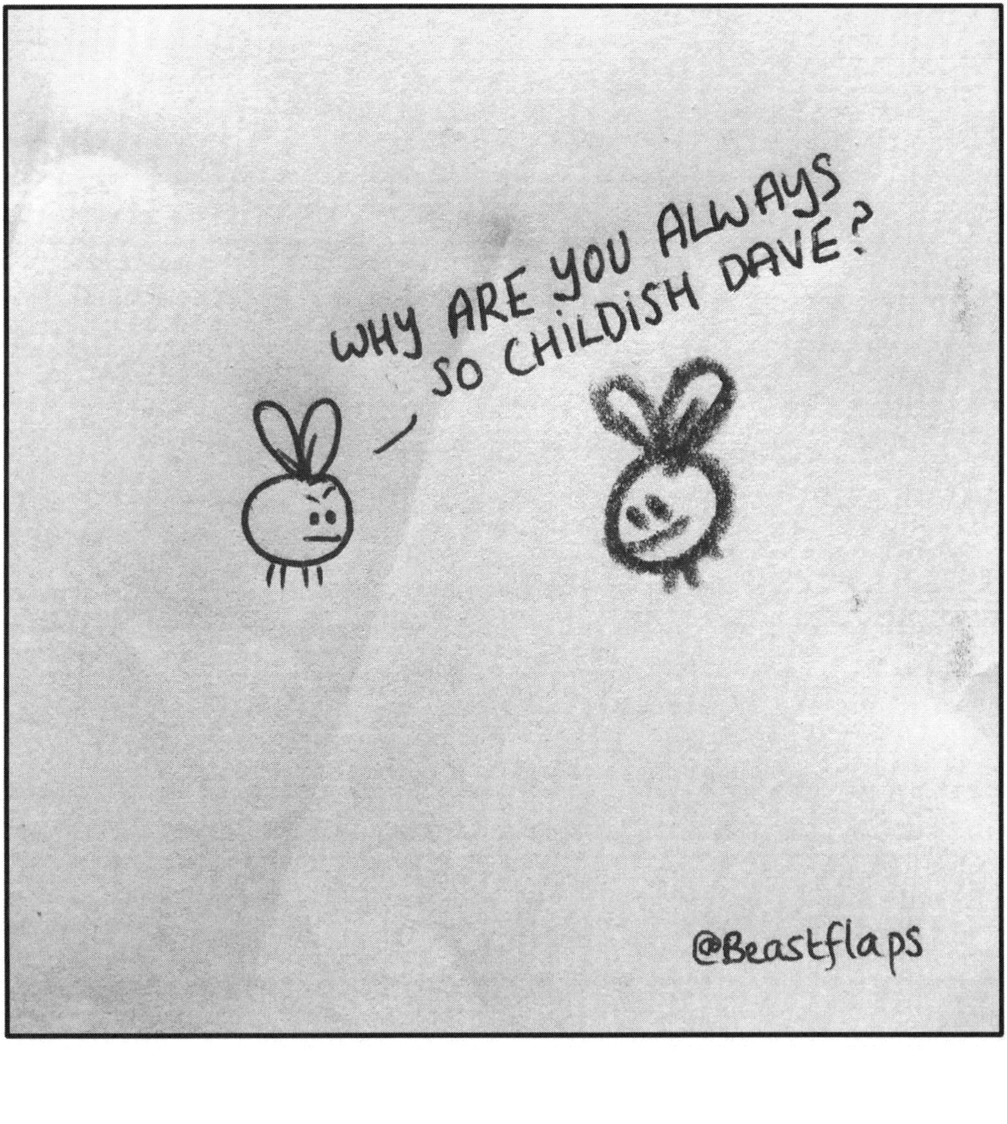
WHY ARE YOU ALWAYS SO CHILDISH DAVE?
@Beastflaps

HERE SHE IS, ALRIGHT LOVELY? WOO-HOO
CHRIST STEVE DO WE HAVE TO DO THIS EVERY TIME? IT'S ME, BARRY.
@Beastflaps

ARE YOU ALMOST DONE BRIAN?
JUST HOLD IT STEADY. THESE THINGS DON'T JUST ASSEMBLE THEMSELVES BARBARA.
@Beastflaps

TAKE YOUR TIME AND JUST LET ME KNOW IF YOU CAN IDENTIFY WHO ATE YOUR HUSBAND
@Beastflaps

YOU KNOW WHAT I JUST DON'T UNDERSTAND DAVE...
EVERYTHING. I'M A FUCKING WORM.
@Beastflaps

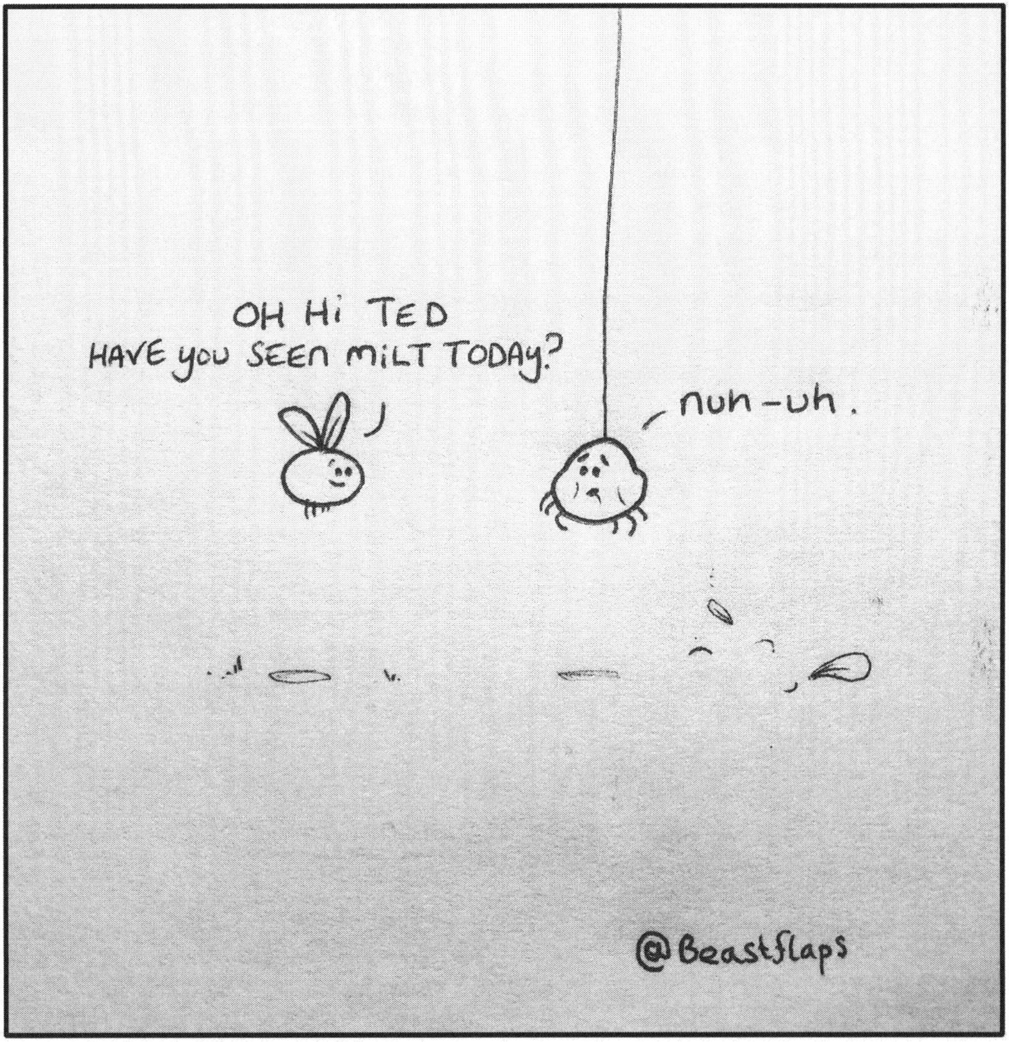
OH Hi TED
HAVE you SEEN MiLT TODAY?
nuh-uh.
@Beastflaps

I LOVE WAKING UP EARLY!

OH LOOK, A BIRD...

@Beastflaps

SO THIS IS NEW YORK HUH?
I EXPECTED A LITTLE MORE
PEZAZ.
@Beastflaps.

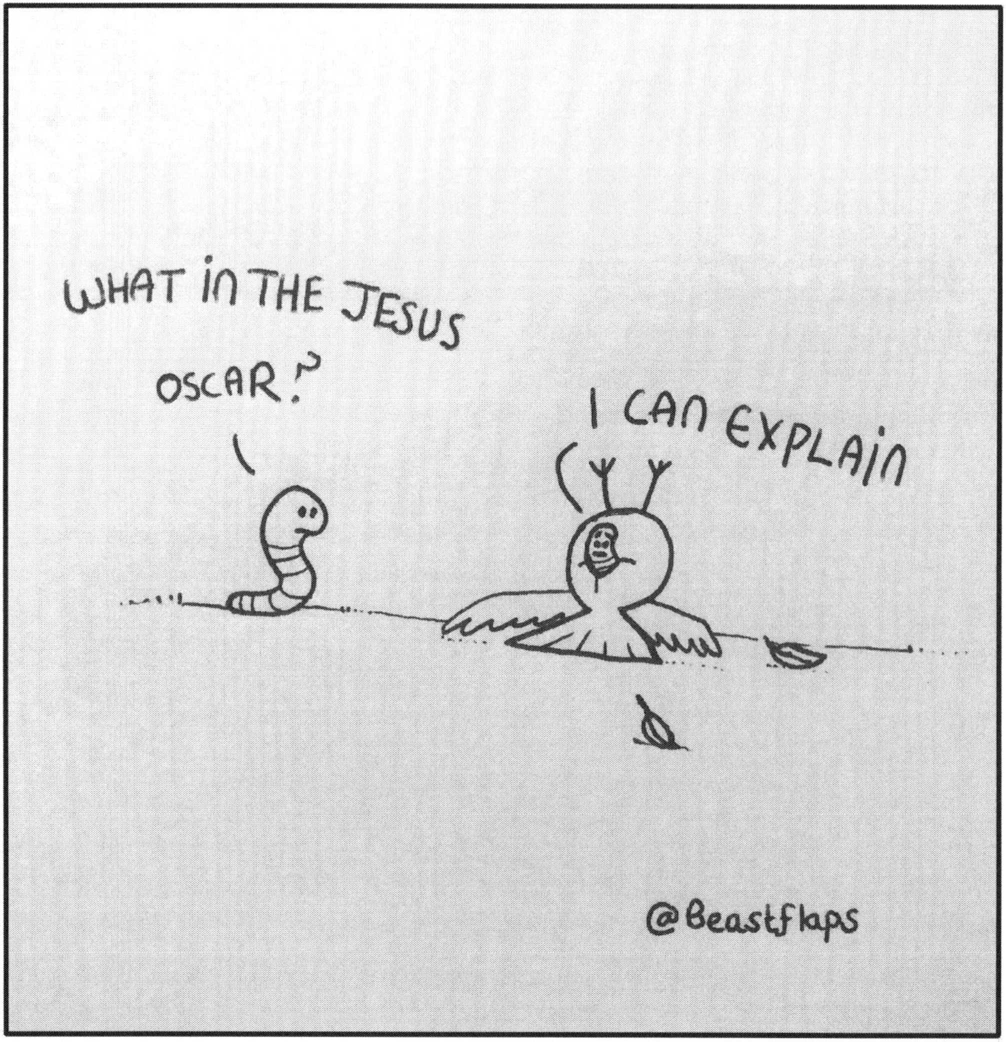
WHAT IN THE JESUS OSCAR!?
I CAN EXPLAIN
@Beastflaps

I LOVE BEING A MAYFLY

CAN'T WAIT UNTIL TOMORROW

@Beastflaps

😠	AN OPEN WINDOW
😊	ANY OTHER WINDOW, AS LONG AS IT'S CLOSED

@Beastflaps

DON'T LOOK AT IT DAVE! IT'S THAT DEADLY LOCUST WAVE THEY'RE TALKING ABOUT
@Beastflaps

DUDE I'M TRYING TO SLEEP
STOP DOING THINGS
SO SORRY
@Beastflaps

LESS CHATTER UP FRONT SMARTASS
♫ WOAH-OH, LEMON ON A PEAR!
@Beastflaps

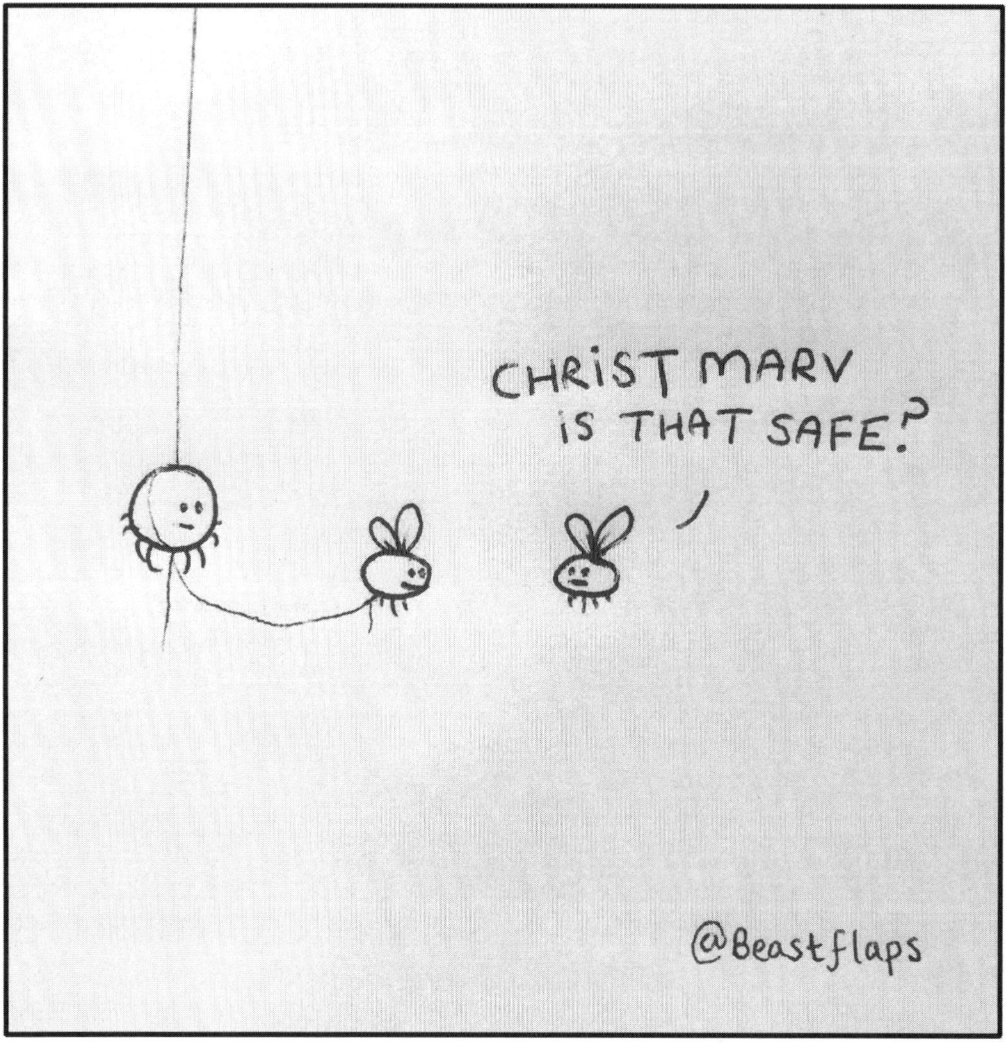
CHRIST MARV
IS THAT SAFE?
@Beastflaps

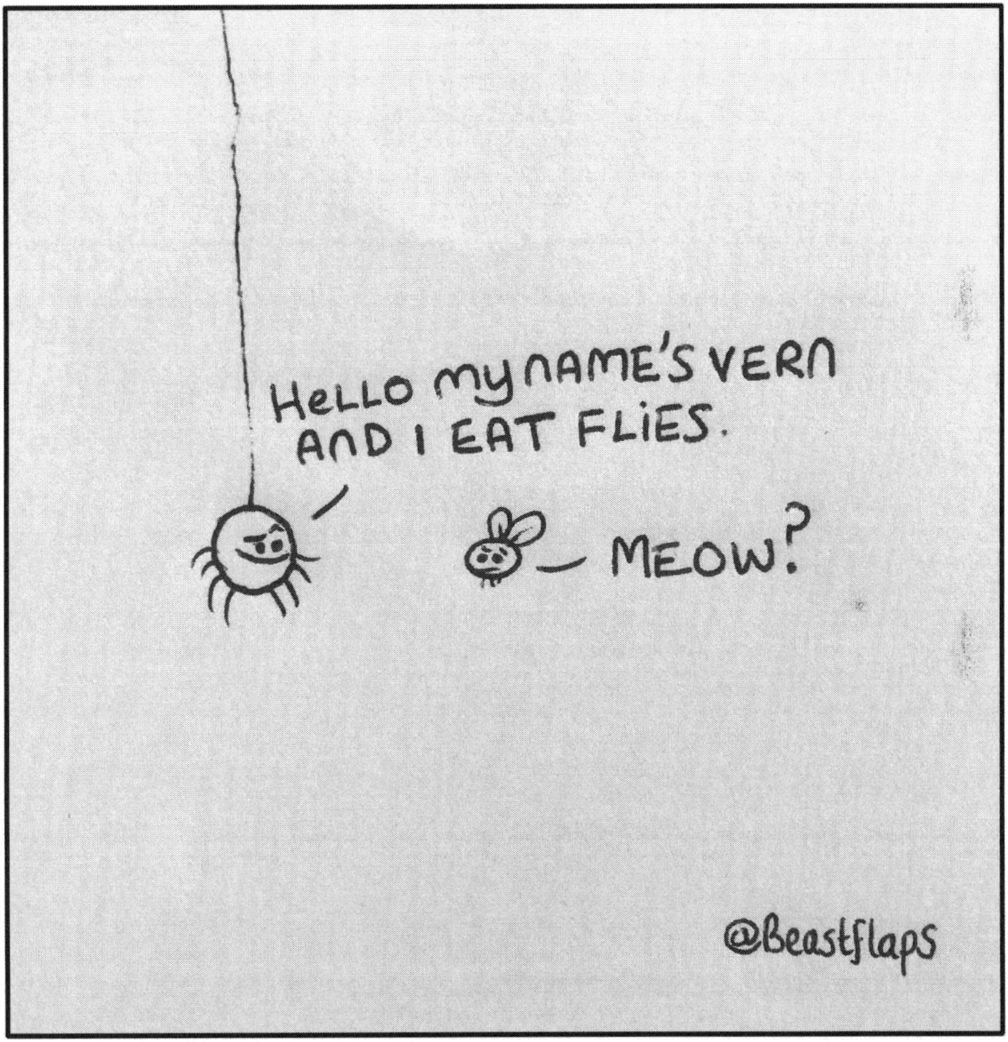
HeLLO my NAME'S VERN AND I EAT FLiES.
MEOW?
@Beastflaps

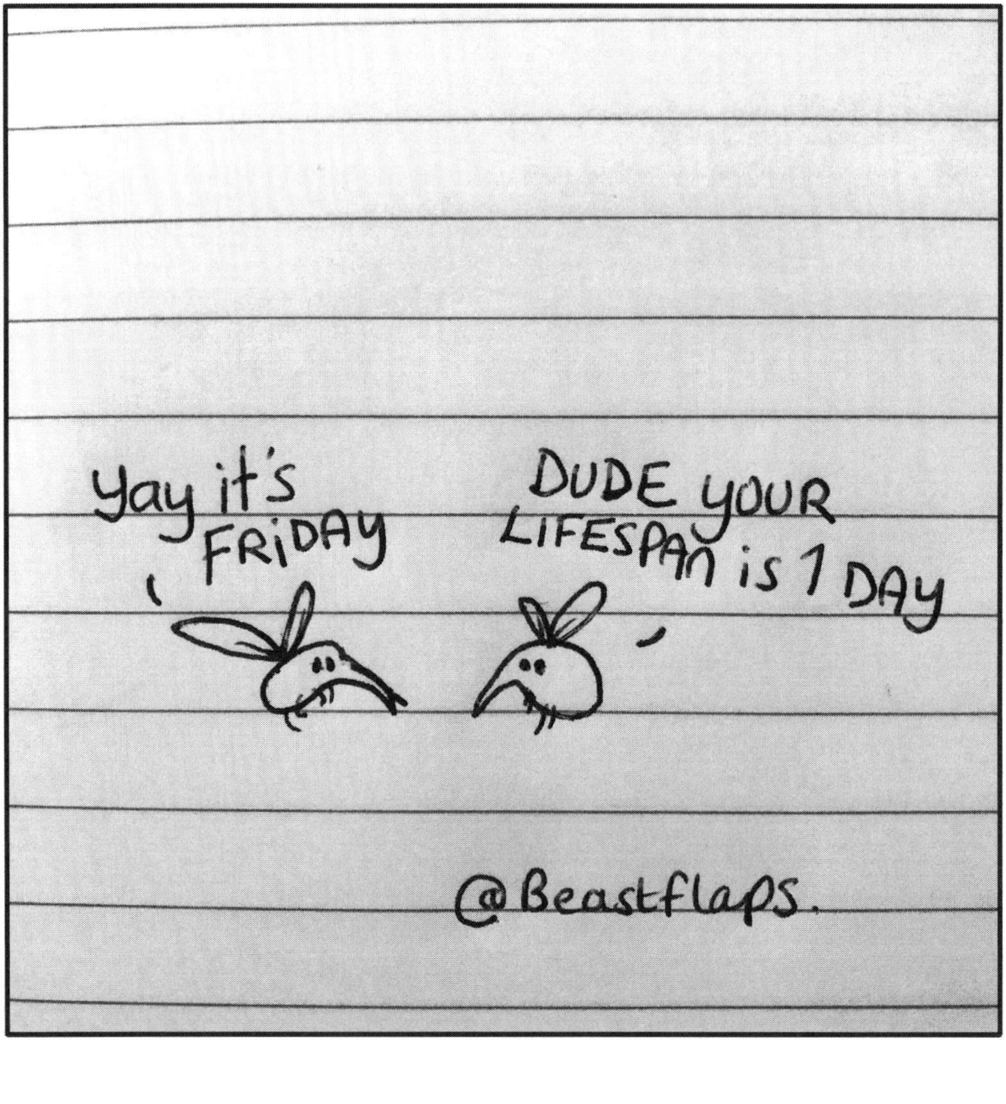
Yay it's FRiDAY
DUDE YOUR LIFESPAN is 1 DAY
@Beastflaps.

I'M FROM A PARALELL UNIVERSE
ONE WHERE THEY CAN'T SPELL?
@Beastflaps

"PRETTY SURE I FOUND THE GIRL FOR ME DAVE."

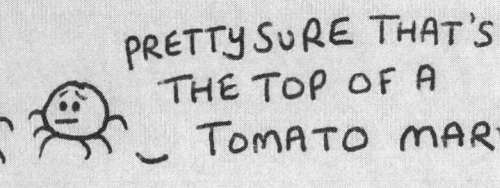

"PRETTY SURE THAT'S THE TOP OF A TOMATO MARV."

@Beastflaps

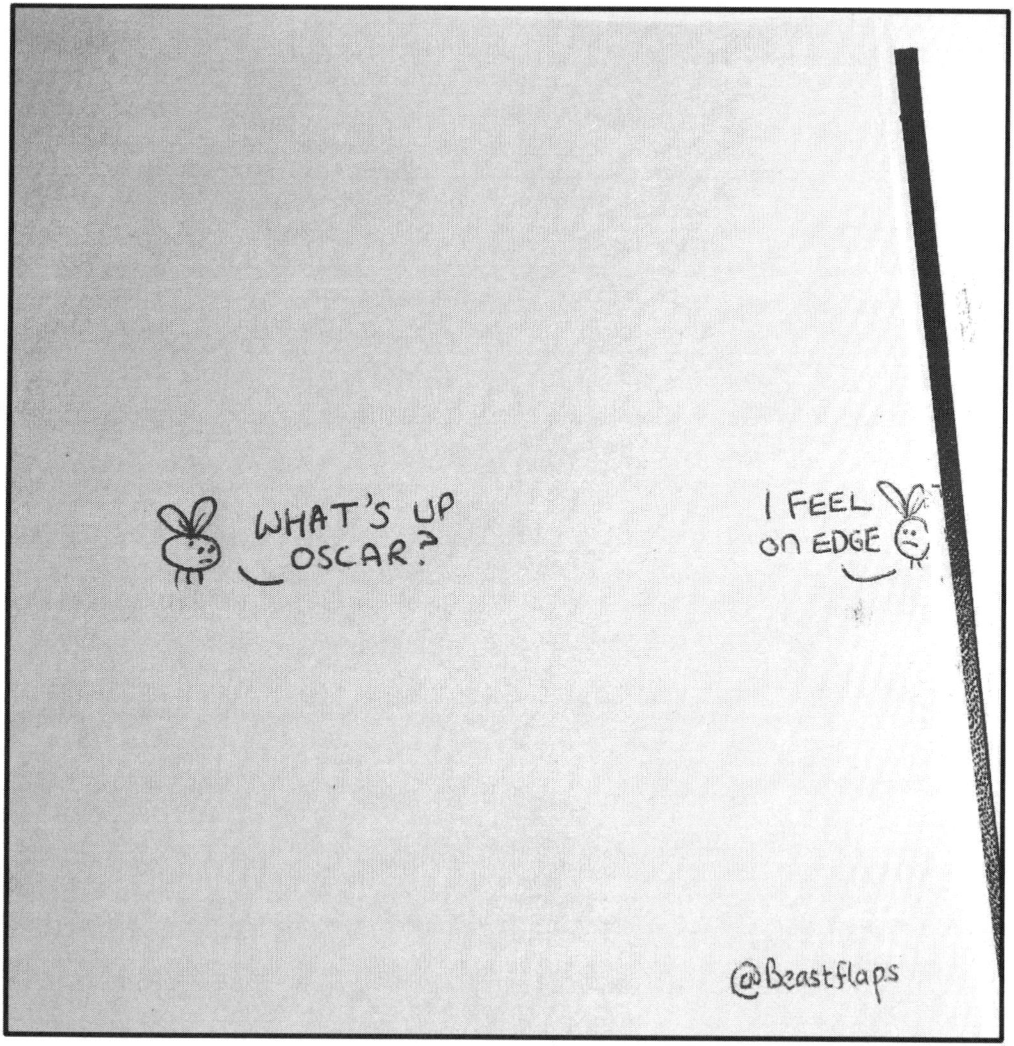
WHAT'S UP OSCAR?
I FEEL ON EDGE
@Beastflaps

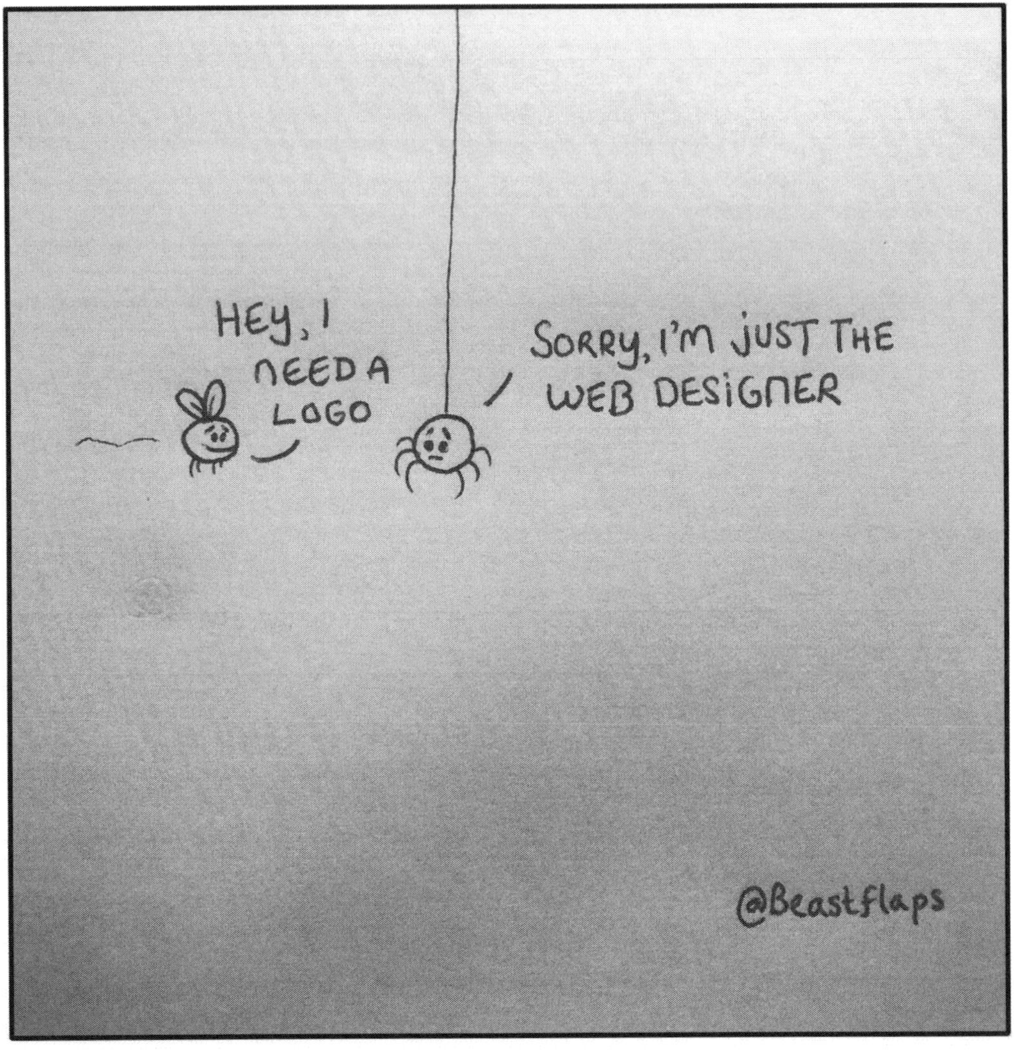
HEY, I NEED A LOGO
SORRY, I'M JUST THE WEB DESIGNER
@Beastflaps

"YOU'RE A GREAT GUY HANK, BUT YOU SUCK WHEN IT COMES TO PEOPLE"

@Beastflaps

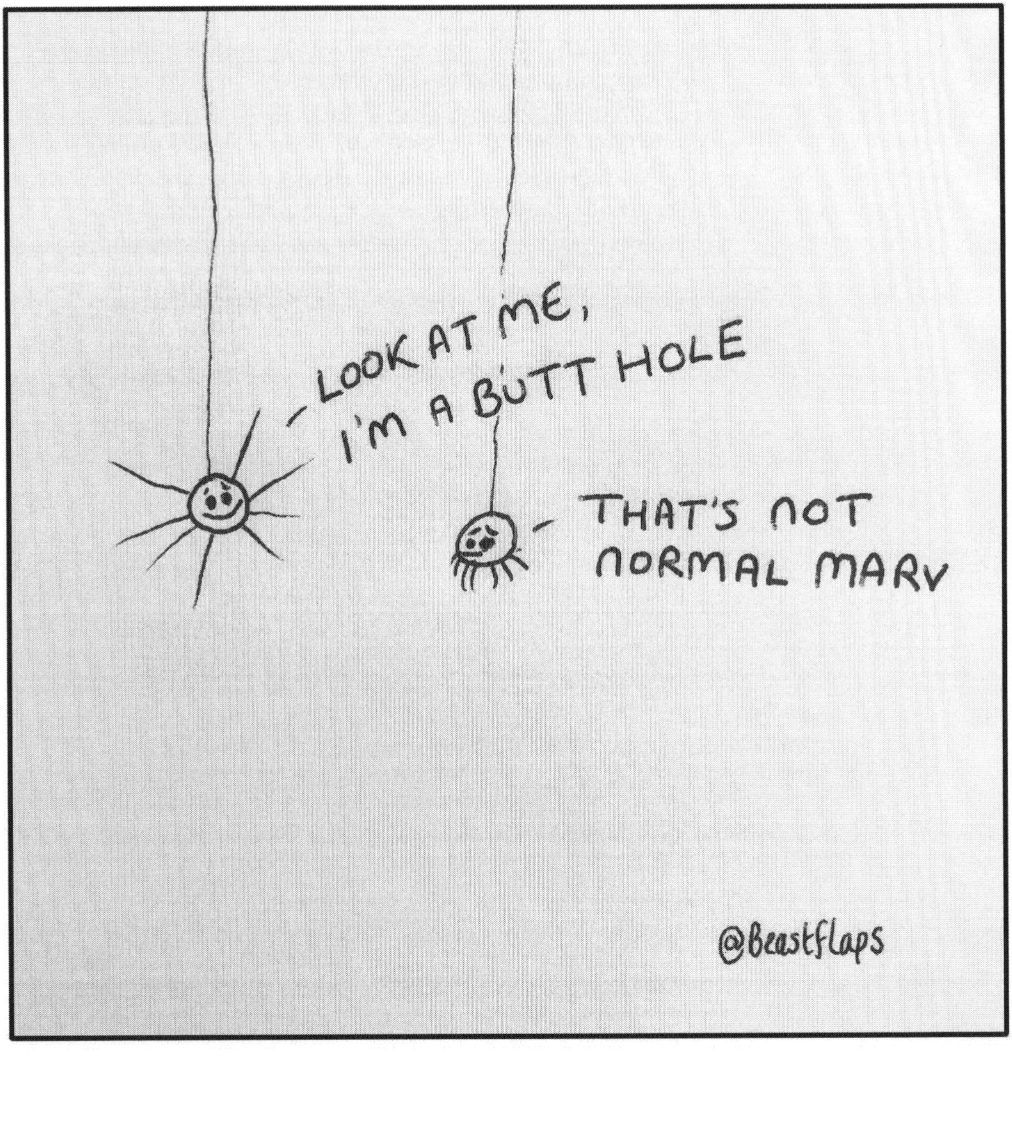
LOOK AT ME,
I'M A BUTT HOLE
THAT'S NOT
NORMAL MARV
@Beastflaps

I'm Finally happy in life, today is the start of a new chapter for me.
@Beastflaps.

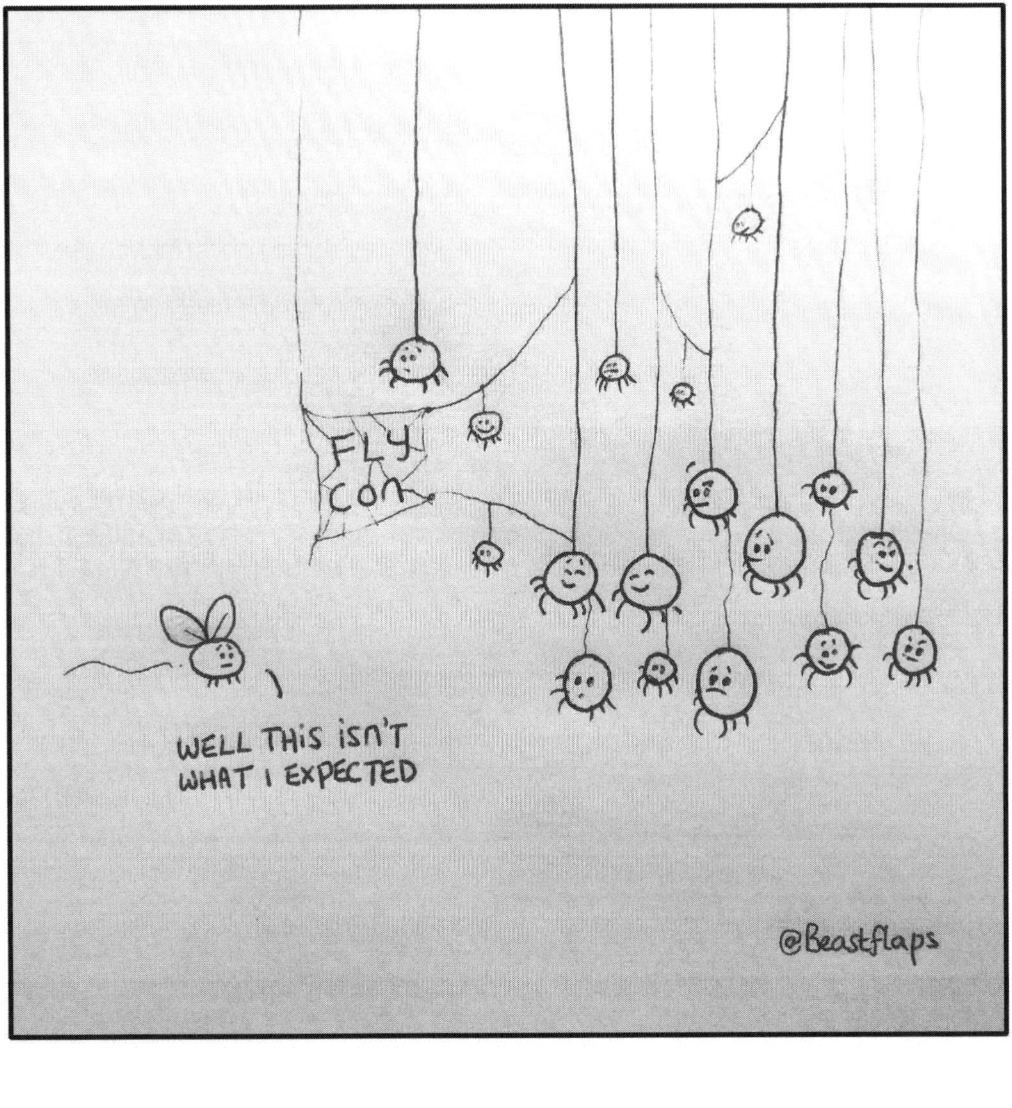
FLY
CON
WELL THIS ISN'T
WHAT I EXPECTED
@Beastflaps

WHAT TOOK YOU SO LONG TO GET OUT OF THE HOUSE?
THEY HAD A SWAT TEAM
@Beastflaps

HEY DAVE WTF is Tony's PROBLEM - HE SWUNG RIGHT PAST ME. DO WE ALL JUST LOOK THE SAME TO YOU NOW?
THAT'S NOT TONY, IT'S BRIAN... AND I'M HIS WIFE BARBARA.
@Beastflaps

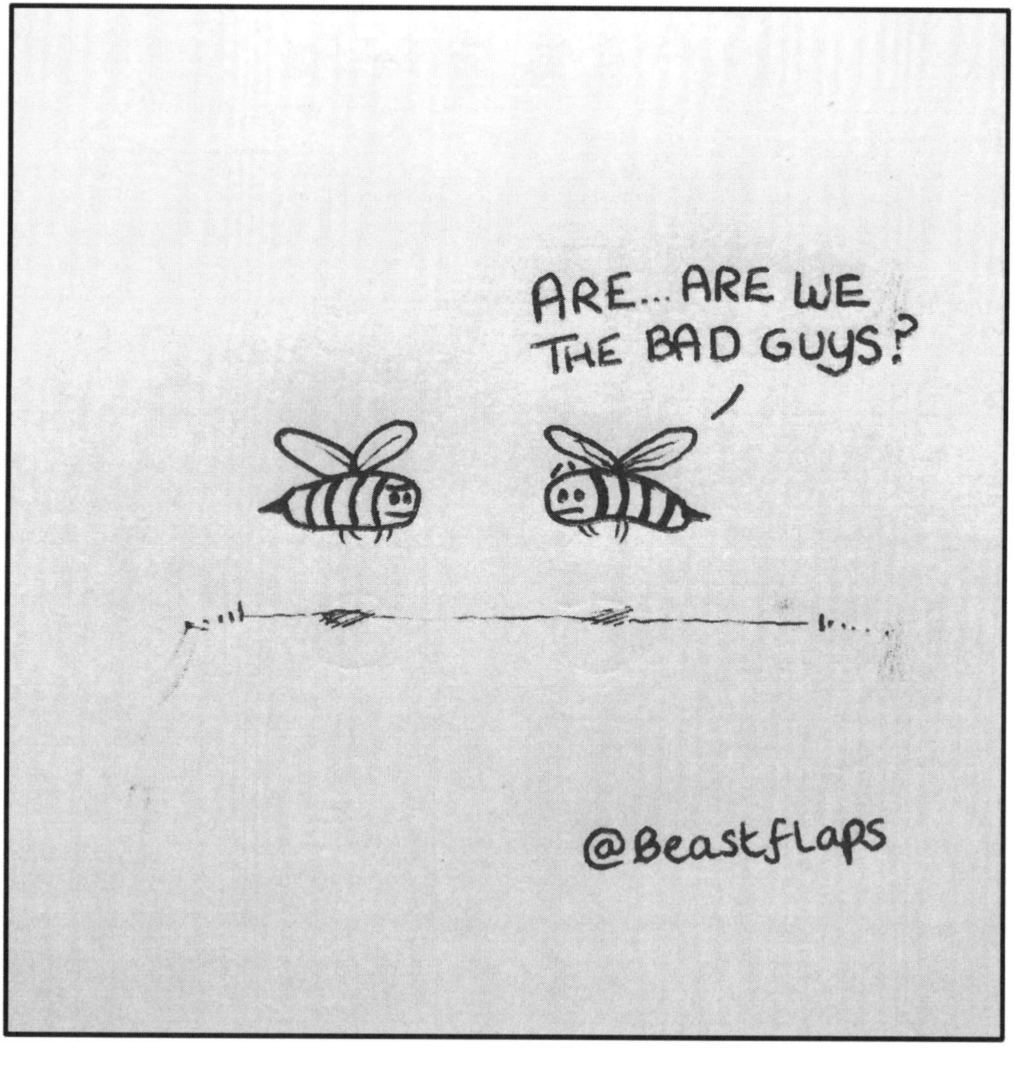
ARE... ARE WE THE BAD GUYS?
@Beastflaps

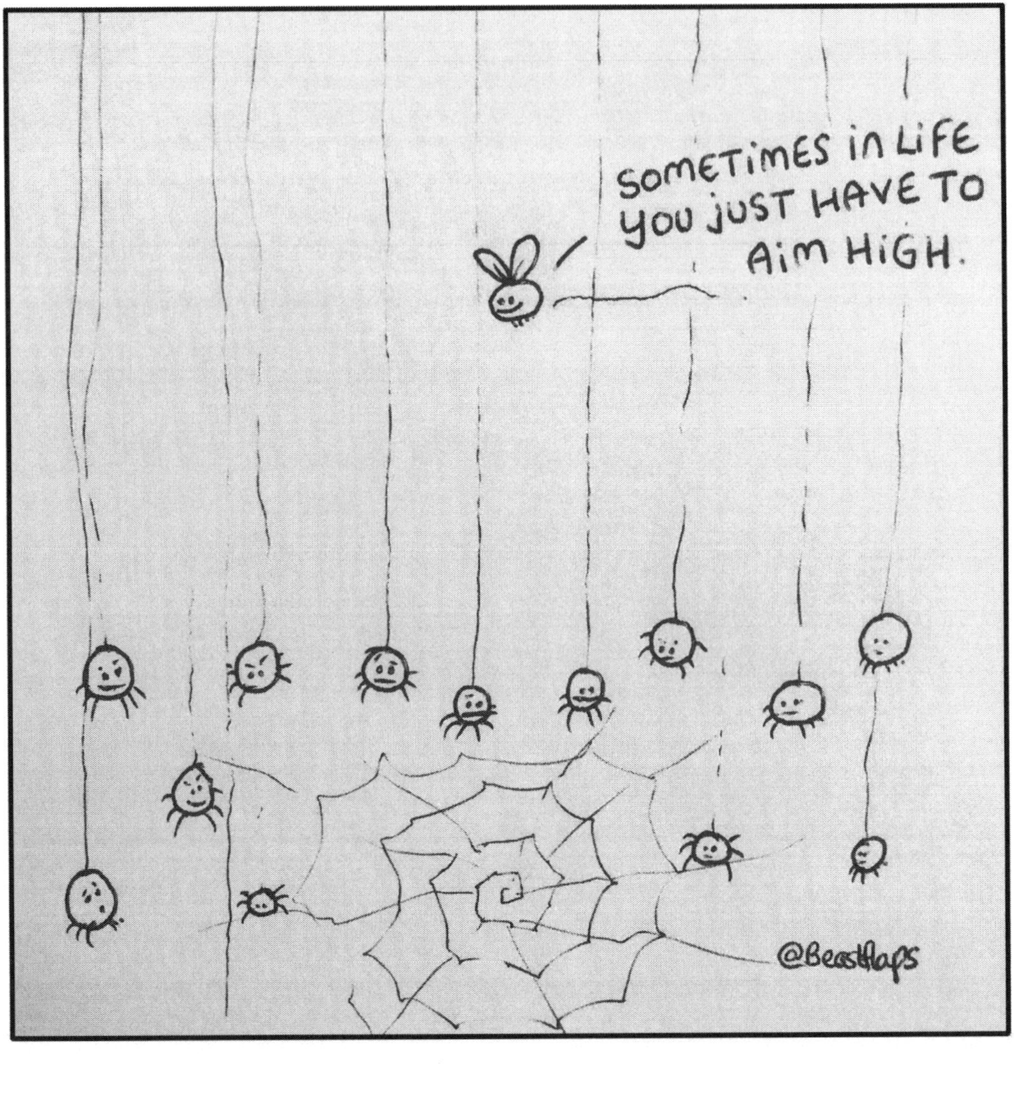
SOMETIMES IN LIFE YOU JUST HAVE TO AIM HIGH.
@BeastFlaps

"WHY SO SERIOUS ALL THE TIME OSCAR?"

@Beastflaps

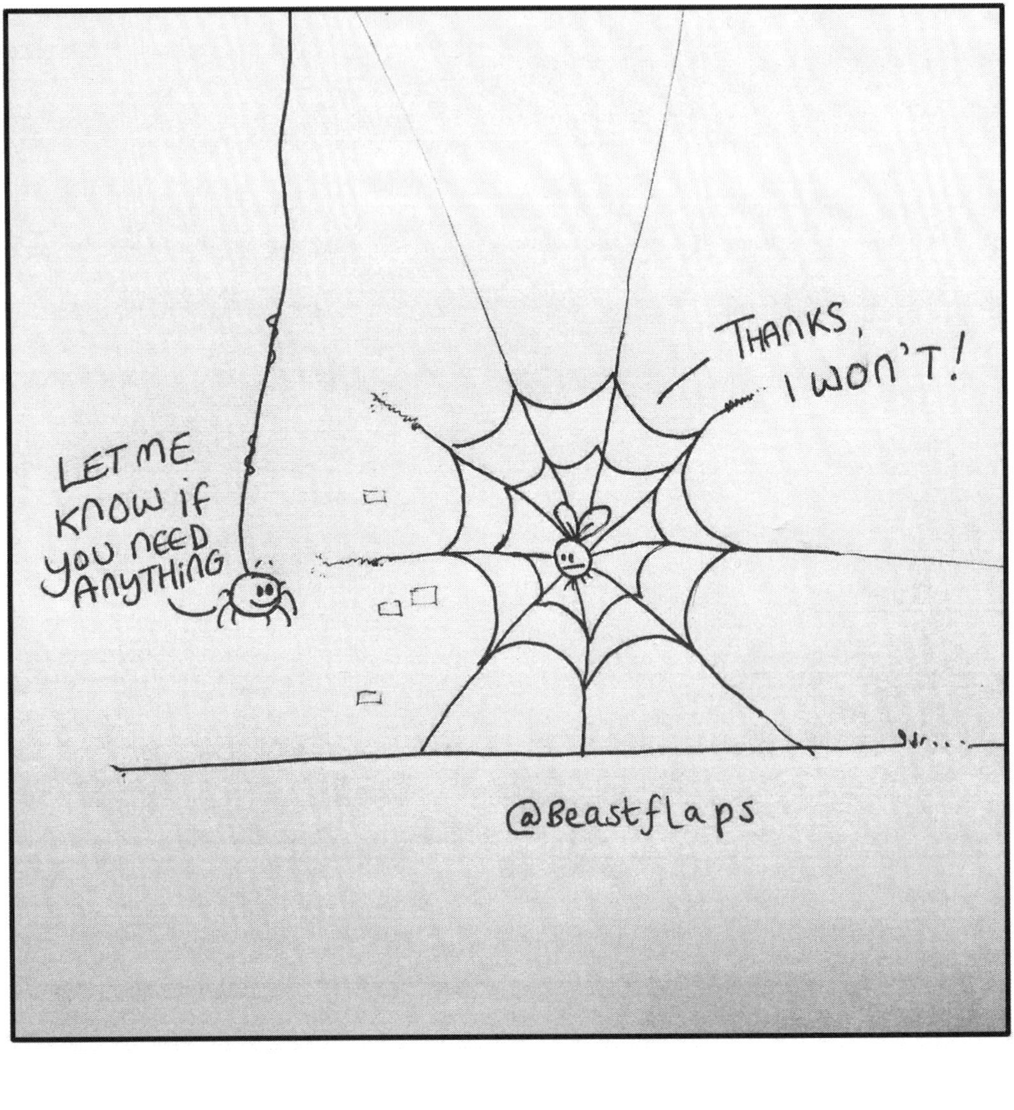
LET ME KNOW IF YOU NEED ANYTHING
THANKS, I WON'T!
@Beastflaps

I'm JUST HAPPY TO FINALLY HAVE A FRIEND, EVEN IF YOU ARE A FUNNY LOOKING FLY.
@Beastflaps

YOUR'E GETTING WARMER!
AH JEEZ MARV I TOLD YOU NOT TO GO TOO FAR, COME ON WILL 'YA?
@Beastflaps

June 2020

22 Monday
(174 - 192)

23 Tuesday
(175 - 191)

24 Wednesday

@Beastflaps

I DON'T GIVE A FUCK WHAT BRIAN SAYS DAVE, MOSQUITOES CAN'T BE VEGAN.
@Beastflaps

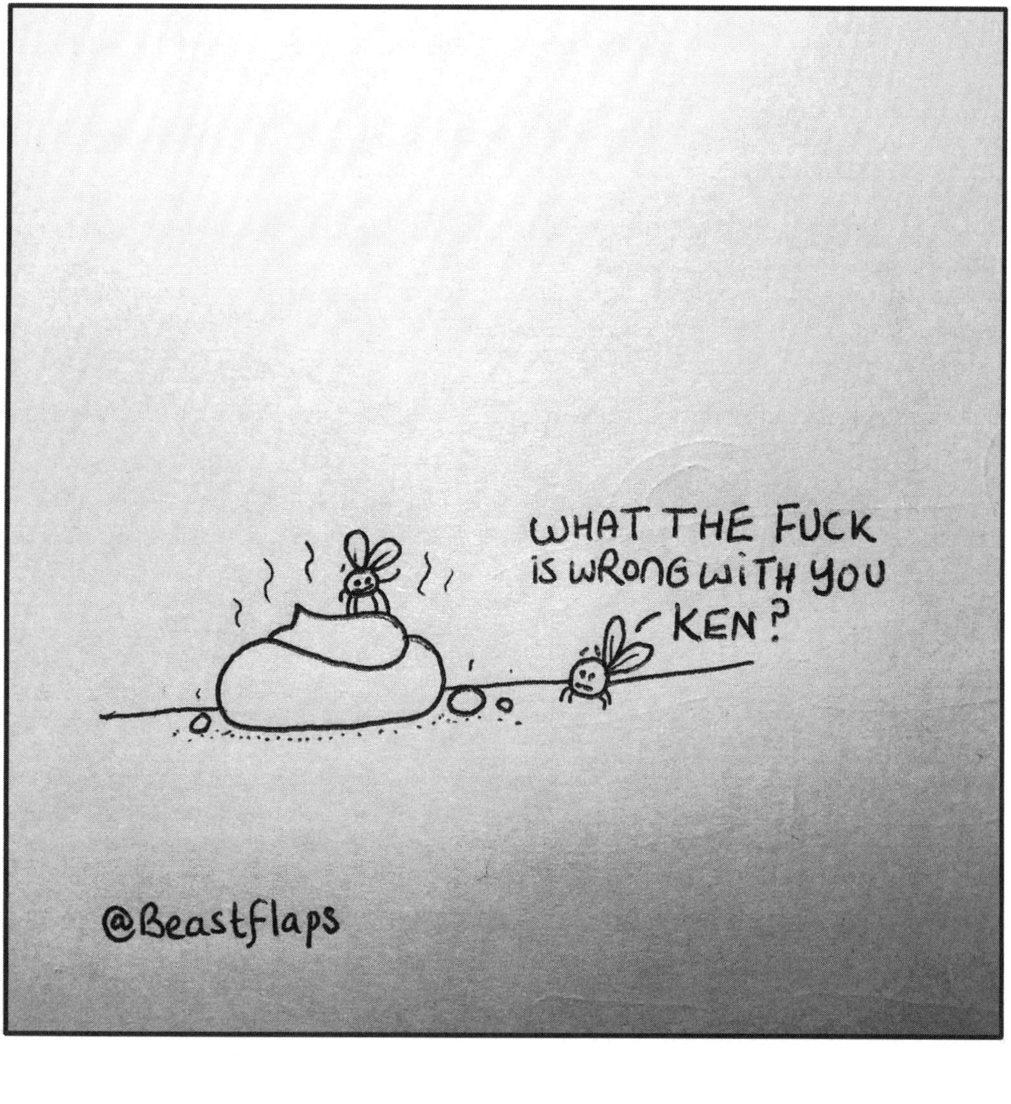
WHAT THE FUCK IS WRONG WITH YOU KEN?
@Beastflaps

I FEEL LIKE YOU DON'T TAKE YOUR ROLE HERE SERIOUSLY ENOUGH HENDERSON
@Beastflaps

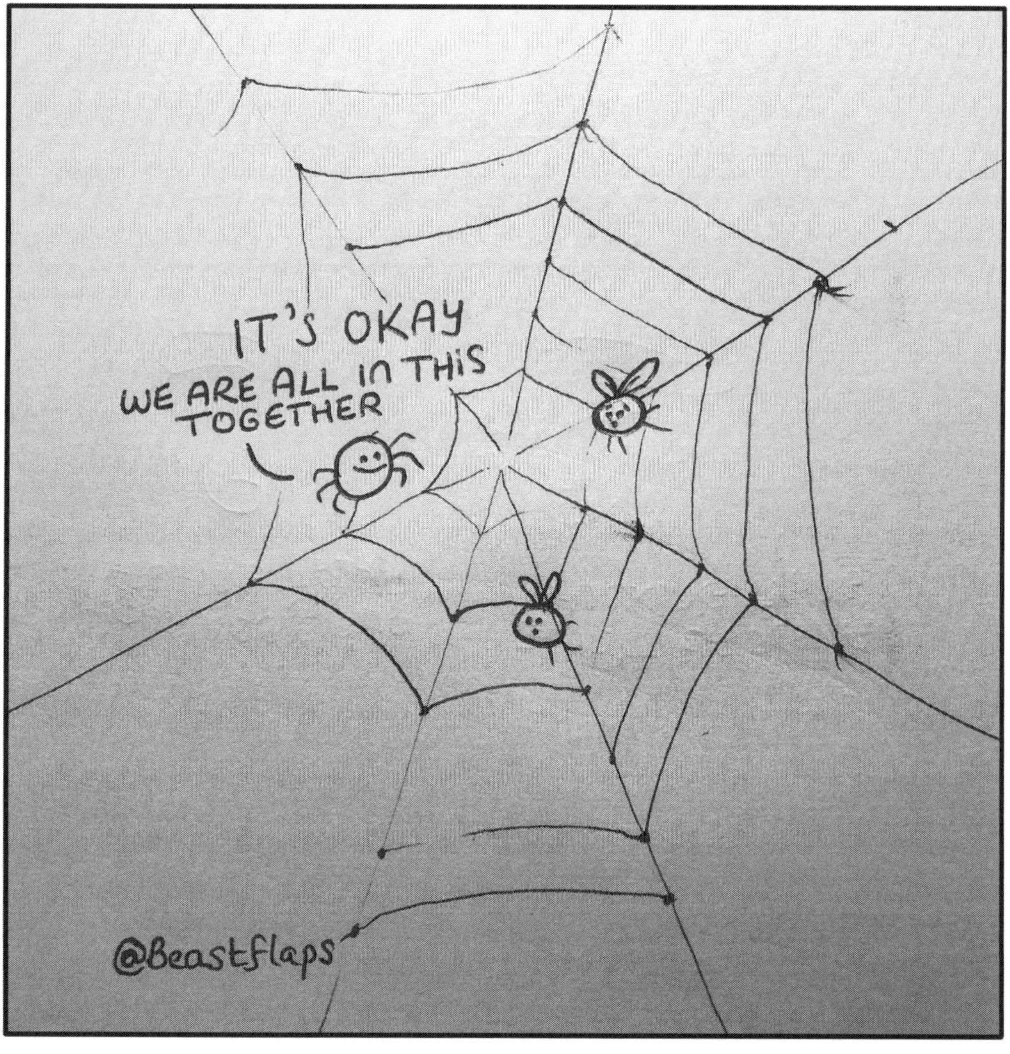
IT'S OKAY
WE ARE ALL IN THIS TOGETHER
@Beastflaps

WHAT ARE YOU DOING KEITH?
I'M GETTING MY SHIT TOGETHER.
@Beastflaps

@Beastflaps
WHAT THE FUCK -ARE YOU DOING DOWN THERE BRIAN?
-HELP

WANNA COME WITH ME AND STEVE AND BASH OURSELVES REPEATEDLY AGAINST THE WINDOW?

@Beastflaps

WANNA COME CRAWL INTO PEOPLE'S MOUTHS AS THEY SLEEP?
WAIT, WE ACTUALLY DO THAT?
@Beastflaps

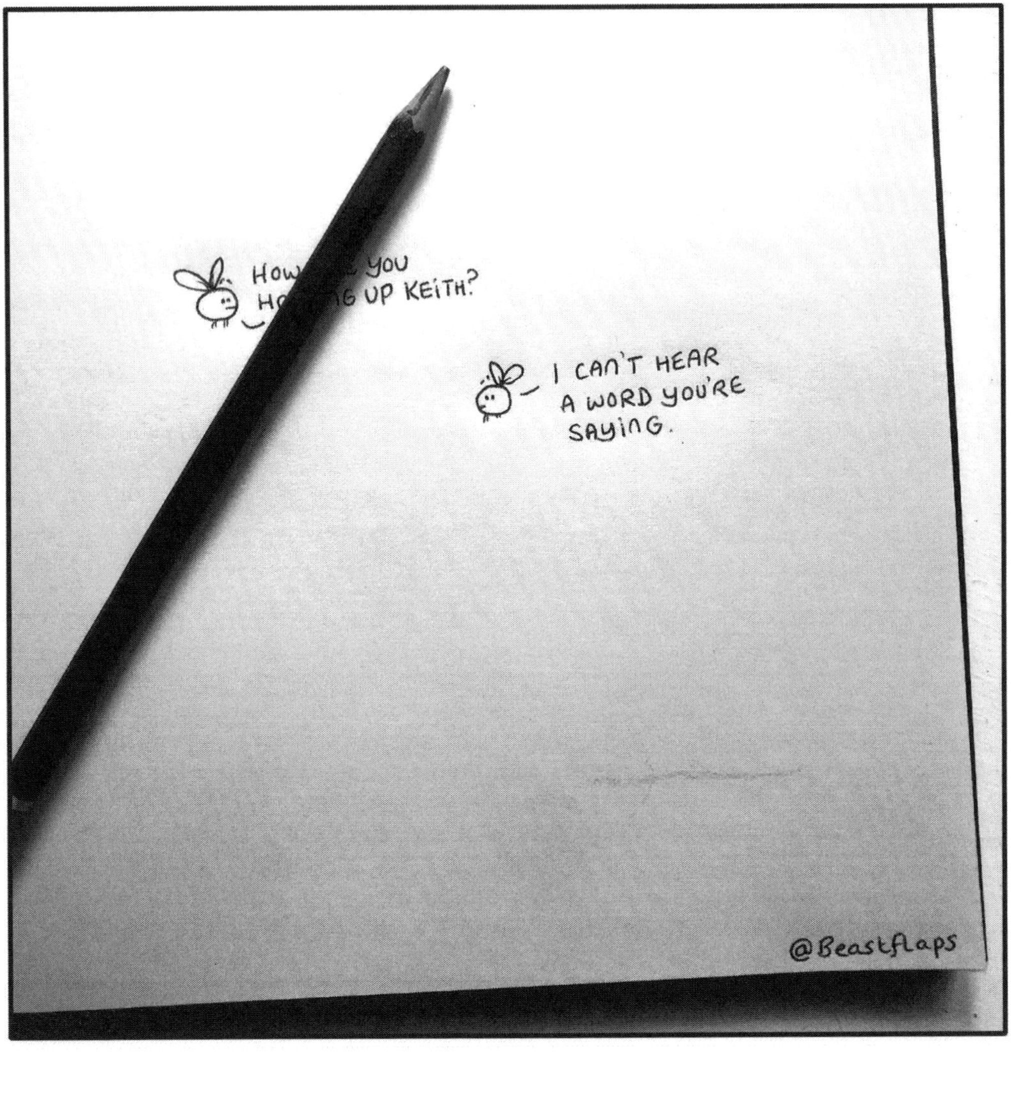
HOW YOU
UP KEITH?
I CAN'T HEAR A WORD YOU'RE SAYING.
@Beastflaps

YOU FUCKING ROCK.
THANK YOU
OH YOU'RE ALIVE. I THOUGHT YOU WERE A ROCK.
@Beastflaps.

HEY STEVE, WANT TO COME WALK TOO CLOSE TO THE HORSE'S EYEBALLS?
MAN, ARE YOU SERIOUS, THAT'S MY THING!
@Beastflaps.

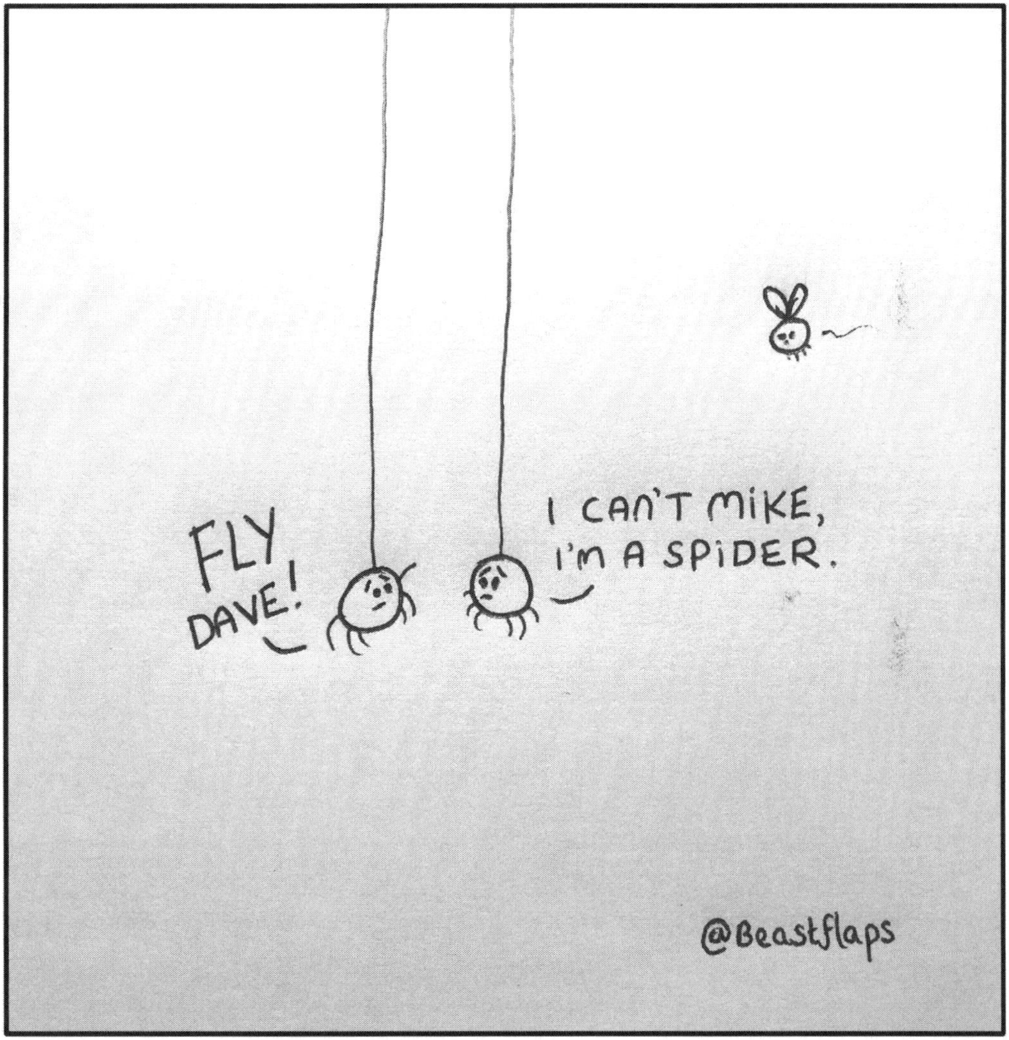
FLY DAVE!
I CAN'T MIKE, I'M A SPIDER.
@Beastflaps

"SORRY TO HEAR ABOUT YOUR OLD MAN. WHAT HAPPENED?"

CYCLIST'S TOOTH

@Beastflaps

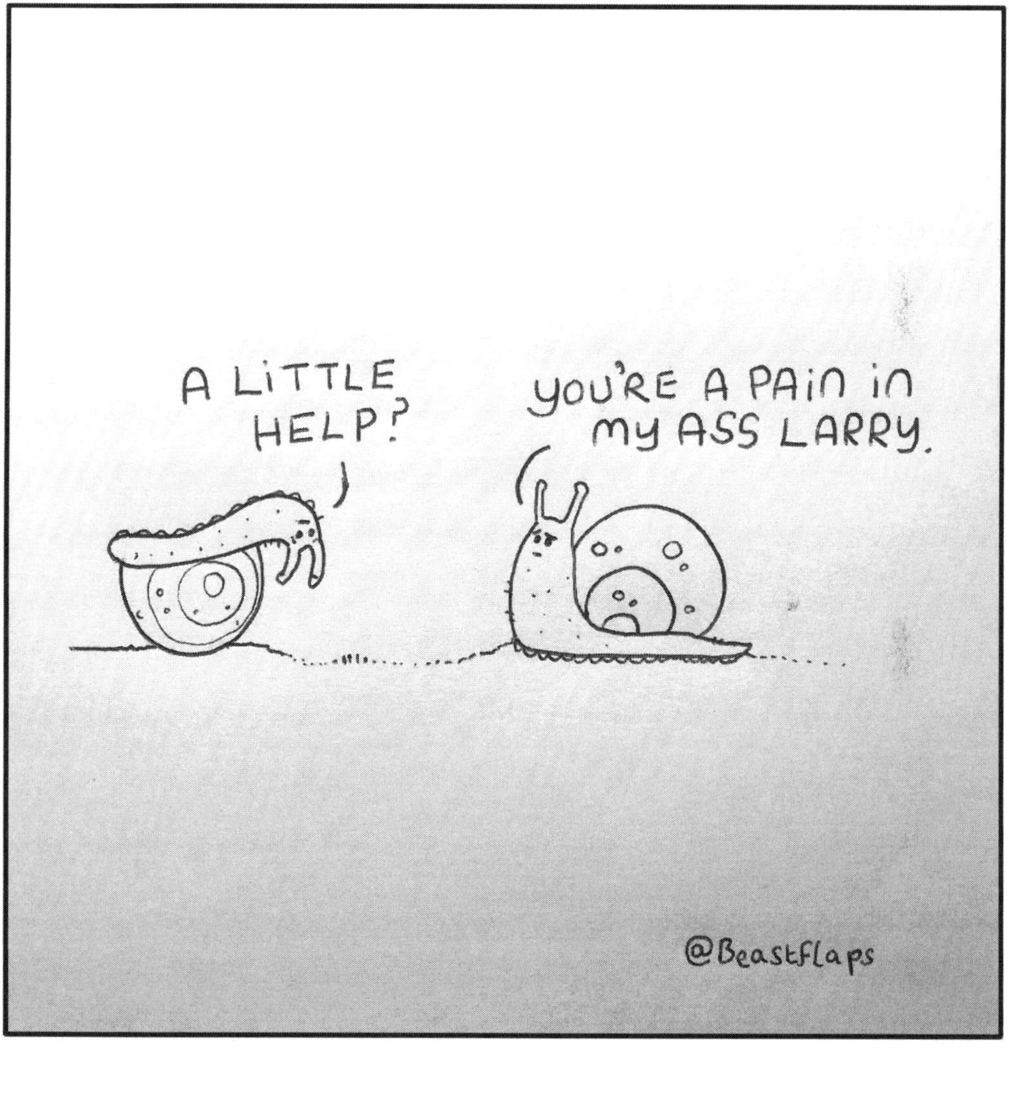
A LITTLE HELP?
YOU'RE A PAIN IN MY ASS LARRY.
@Beastflaps

QUICK STEVE, TURN BACK. A SPIDER JUST CAUGHT MY COUSIN
WHO, RAY?
THIS IS NO TIME TO CHEER, STEVE.
@Beastflaps

CAREFUL TODAY MIKE, I HEARD THAT ONE OF THE GUYS IS AN OWL IN DISGUISE.

WHO?

@Beastflaps

HAVE YOU GOT NOTHING BETTER TO DO THAN HANG OUT WITH YOUR FRIENDS ON THE WEB ALL DAY?
I'M GONNA SAY NO?
@Beastflaps

"Time's fun when you're having flies."

@Beastflaps

I JUST CAN'T SHAKE THE FEELING THAT EVERYONE'S OUT TO GET ME, DOC.
@beastflaps

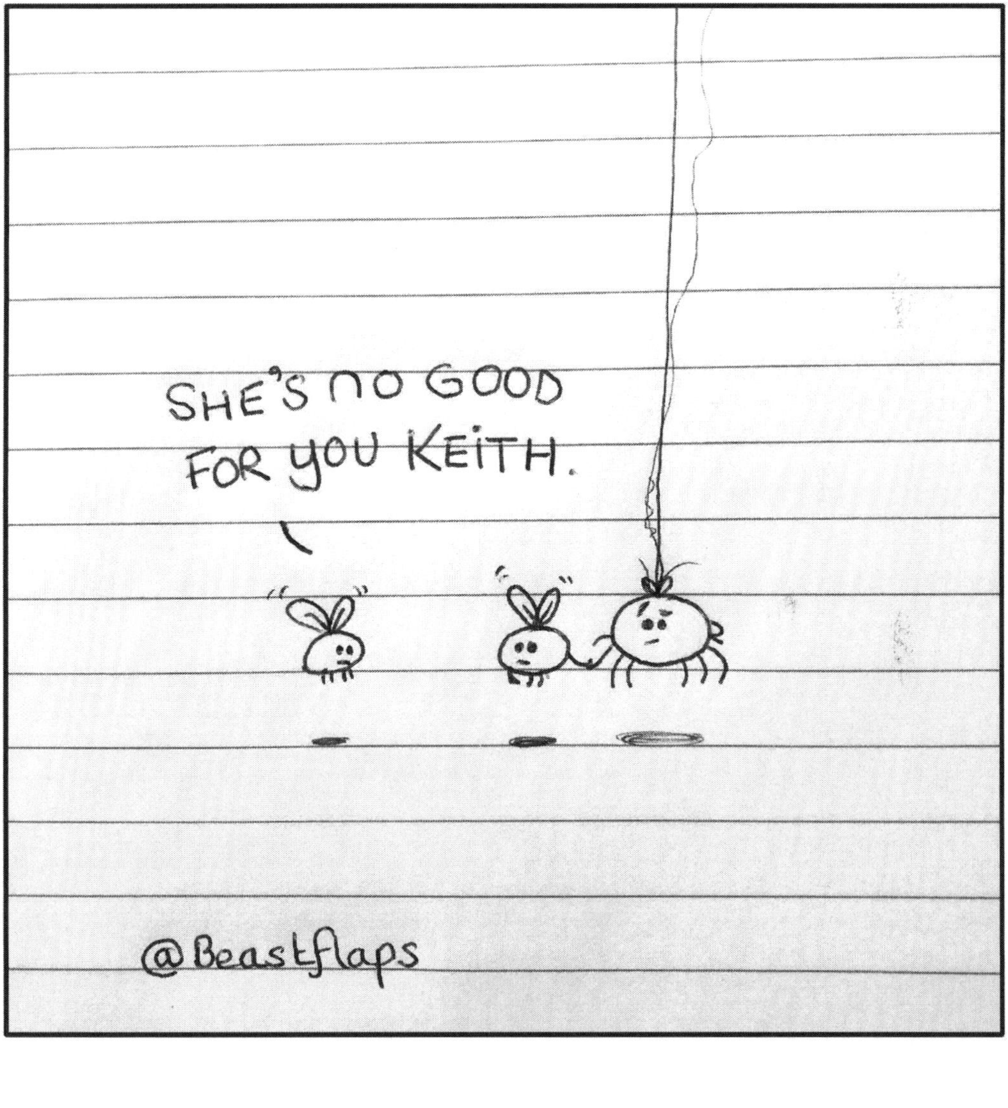
SHE'S no GOOD
FOR you KEITH.
@Beastflaps

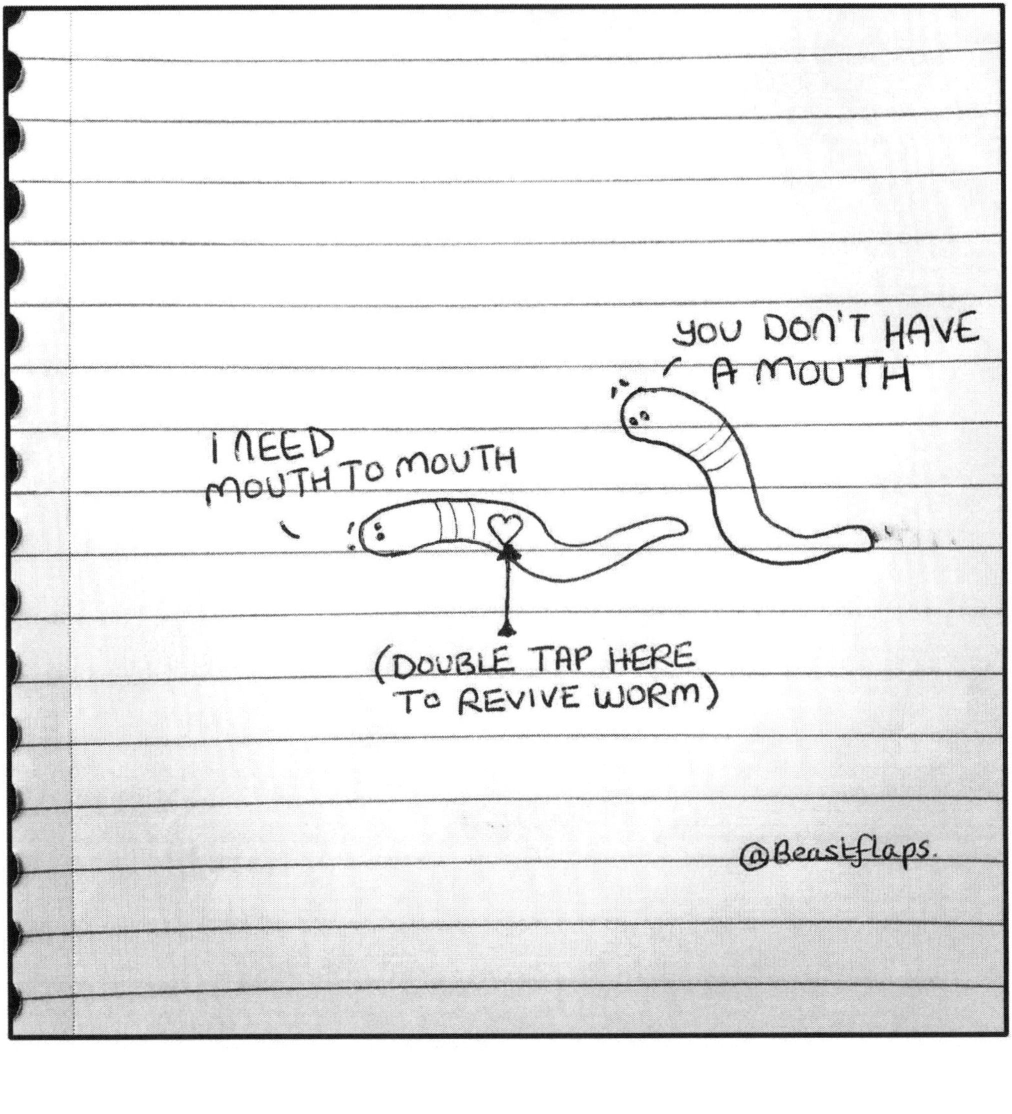
YOU DON'T HAVE A MOUTH
I NEED MOUTH TO MOUTH
(DOUBLE TAP HERE TO REVIVE WORM)
@Beastflaps.

SERIOUSLY MAN WHAT THE FUCK'S WITH THAT NOISE IT'S 3.A.M.
NO COMPRENDE

CAN YOU HEAR THAT DAMNED BUZZING VERN OR IS IT JUST ME?
@beastflaps

HI, MY NAME'S DAVE AND I HAVEN'T HAD AN URGE TO EAT ANYONE SINCE 8 A.M ON TUESDAY
BUT TODAY IS TUESDAY...
...AAAND IT'S NOW 8:04
@Beastflaps

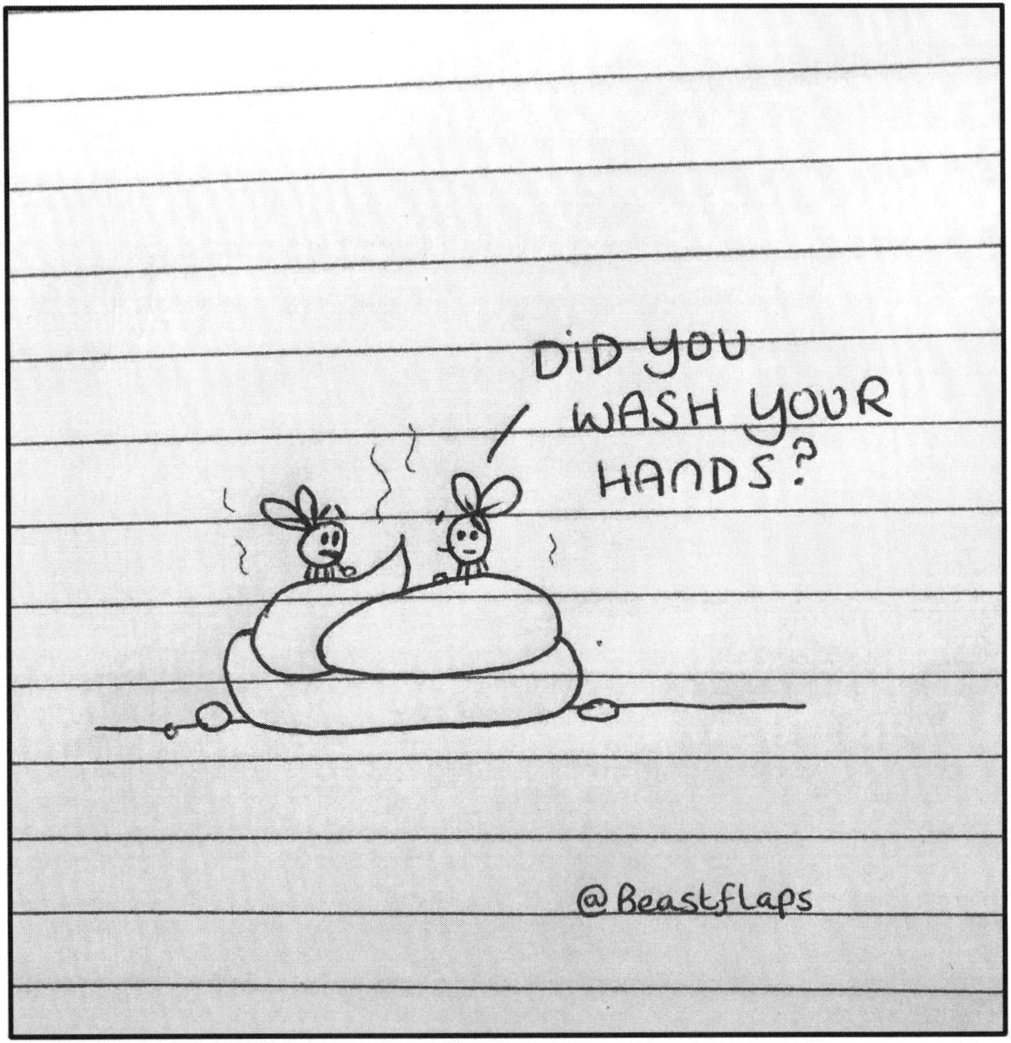
DID YOU
WASH YOUR
HANDS?
@Beastflaps

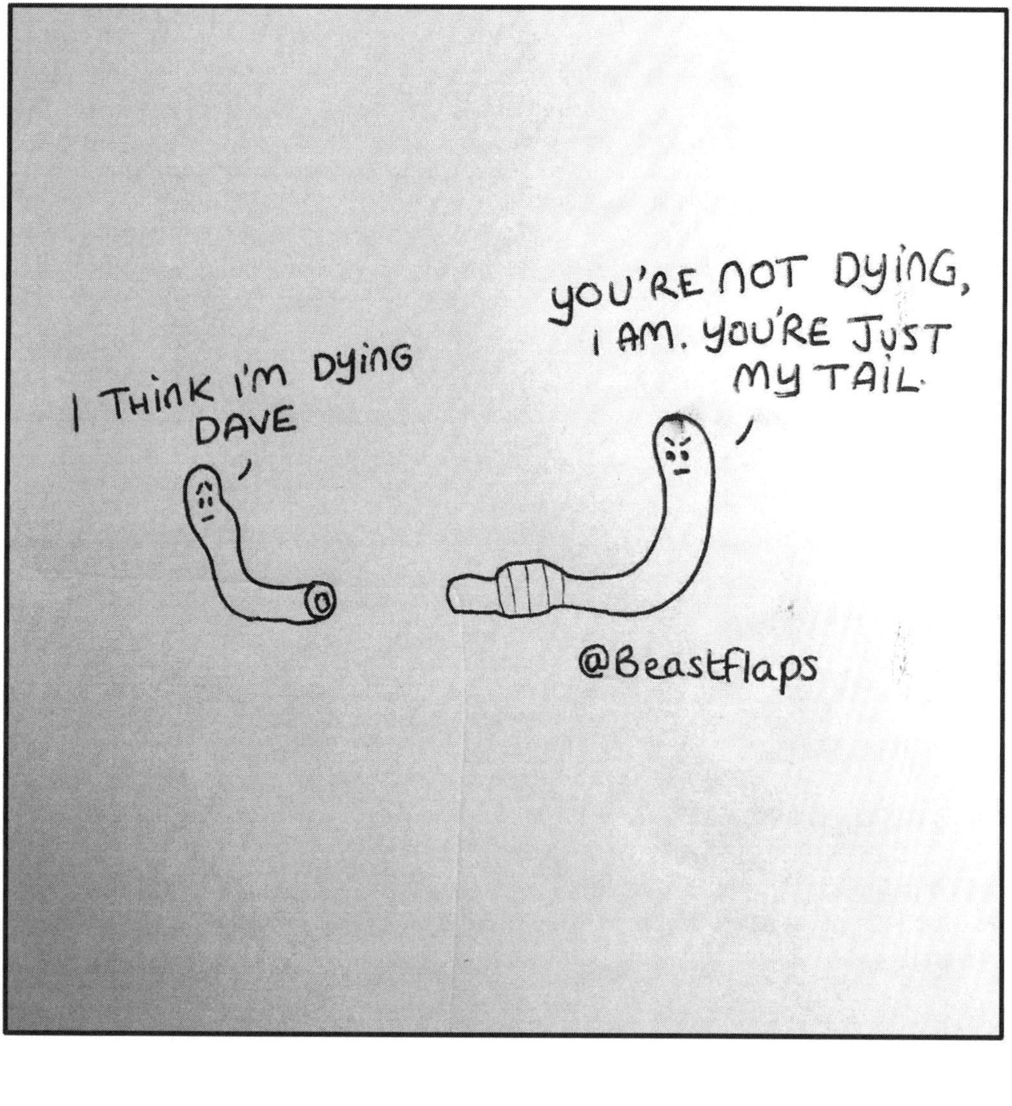
I THINK I'M DYING DAVE
YOU'RE NOT DYING, I AM. YOU'RE JUST MY TAIL.
@Beastflaps

WHEW, LOOKS LIKE I FINALLY OUTRAN THAT STUPID SPIDER!
@Beastflaps

DAD, I HAVE SOME WEIRD PATTERNS COMING OUT OF MY BUTT
AH YES, WELL THAT'S ERM, IT'S... WHERE'S YOUR MOTHER? BARBARA!?
@BeastFlaps

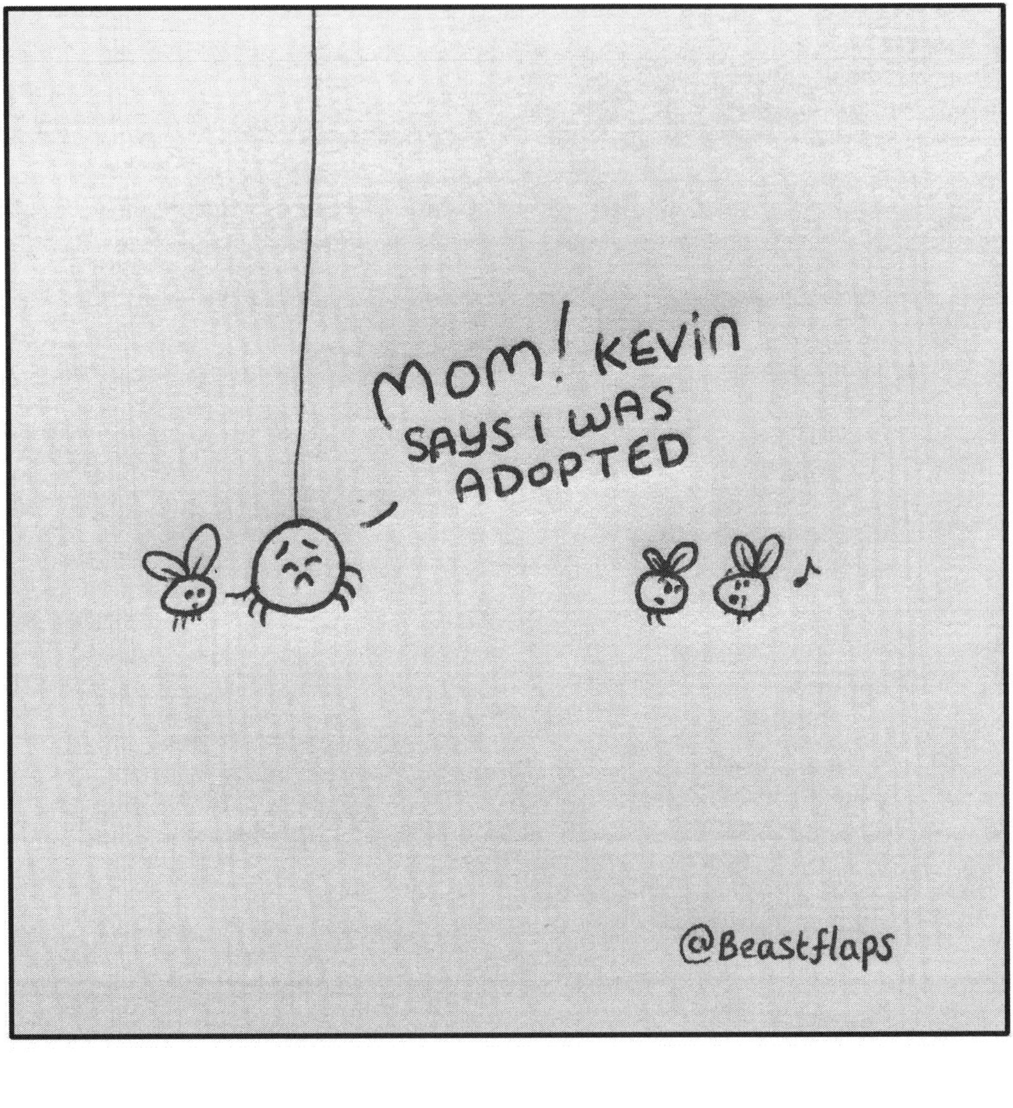
MOM! KEVIN SAYS I WAS ADOPTED
@Beastflaps

YOUR FRIEND WAS A LITTLE RUDE TO ME THIS MORNING
DUDE, HE'S A SPIDER. YOU'RE LUCKY HE DIDN'T SUCK YOUR INSIDES OUT THROUGH YOUR ASSHOLE.
@Beastflaps

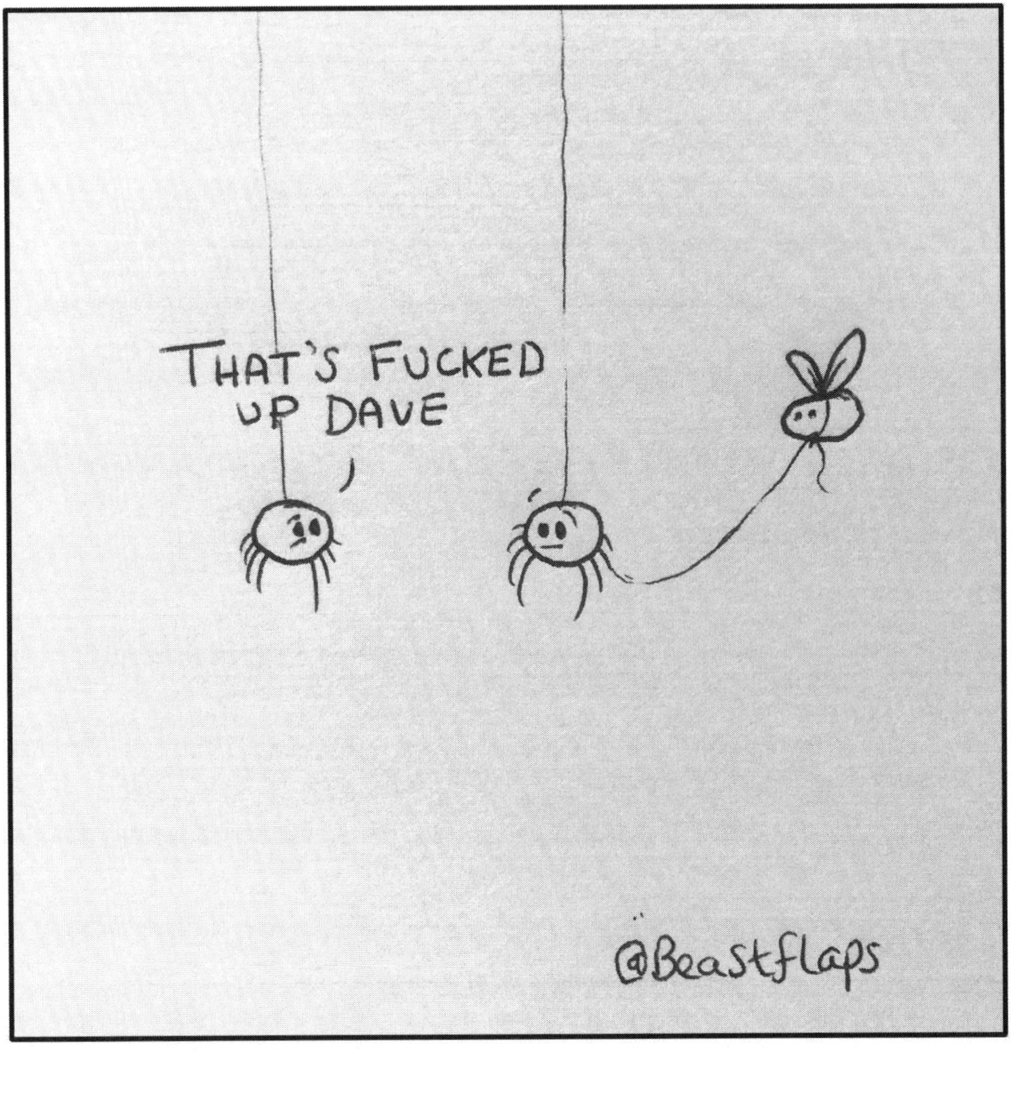
THAT'S FUCKED UP DAVE
@Beastflaps

Fin.

BugDoodles.com

Printed in Great Britain
by Amazon